Nightmare on the Nightshift

Colin Goodwin

First Edition published 2019 by

2QT Limited (Publishing)

Settle, North Yorkshire United Kingdom

This is a work of fiction and any resemblance to any person
living or dead is purely coincidental. The place names
mentioned are real but have no connection with
the events in this book

Cover Design by Charlotte Mouncey

Printed in Great Britain by Ingram Spark UK Ltd

A CIP catalogue record for this book is
available from the British Library

ISBN 978-1-913071-11-0

Nightmare
on the
Nightshift

A Fairly Grim Tale

A cool, calm and fresh autumn morning on the Leeds and Liverpool Canal; erratic gusts of wind separate millions of crispy leaves from their branches. Unfortunately, one family on their recently hired narrow boat are disturbing the peace.

The lady on this trip had sought solitude at the front of the boat to separate herself from the stink of exhaust fumes, the monotonous clonk of the diesel engine, and the irritating sound of her husband's voice. She was sitting on the cushioned lid of the propane gas locker, pondering. 'It is amazing...just forty feet is the distance between absolute mayhem and total tranquillity,' she thought.

Wearing a windproof jacket, woolly hat and compulsory brightly coloured buoyancy aid, she breathed in the fresh air and stared at the fallen leaves floating on the canal surface. Leaning further over the front of the rusty hull, she watched with fascination as they darted quickly around the prow as if avoiding a collision. It was so quiet and peaceful as they cruised along that she felt rejuvenated just being there. The birds were singing and there wasn't a cloud in the bright blue sky. All she had to remember was… '*Under no circumstances let go of the soddin windlass! Canal bottom's full of 'em!!*'

Those had been her hysterical husband's parting words as she'd walked, lock handle in hand, up the narrow passageway to solitude.

It had seemed a good idea at the time. In the brochure it was described as the most relaxing holiday ever: sunlight glinting on the slow flowing canal; the sound of water lapping against the hull; beautiful countryside at your feet, with access to sleepy villages and the friendship of fellow boaters.

She looked down the boat towards the stern. She could see her husband who, for some strange reason, was sporting a blue roll-neck sweater and captain's hat, complete with anchor motif. She watched as he shouted instructions to their son about the skills of narrow boat handling and demonstrated by pointing at the various controls. Her son looked at him with a bemused expression. Luckily the noise of the big engine drowned out her husband's voice but, annoyingly, even from this distance she could see his barking, wide-open mouth and flapping arms as he instructed his son, who was doing his best to negotiate a bend in the canal.

The engine screamed and canal water sprayed from the rear of the boat as her son opened the throttle too far; then, as he steered too close to the bank, there was an audible bump and a sensation throughout the boat as though he had cruised over an obstacle. The engine slowed down then struggled to keep going as if it were restricted. Then, with a splutter and a cough, it finally gave up and stalled.

Exasperated at his son's obvious incompetence and enveloped in diesel engine smoke, 'Mr Captain' grabbed the tiller handle, switched off the dead engine and steered the drifting, powerless boat to the bank.

'That's it! Something's got wrapped around the prop,' he shouted to his wife, whilst stamping on his hat in a fit of rage.

His son looked towards his mother who smiled, shook her head and mouthed, 'Don't worry.'

They secured the boat to the embankment with mooring spikes and ropes then considered their next move.

'We can't carry on until we have sorted out the prop,' the captain commanded. 'We'll let the engine cool down then after a brew, you and I will go down and open the weed hatch. We'll soon be able to see what the problem is,' he said, pointing at the engine compartment and then at his son.

His son backed away.

'You might as well use this as an opportunity to find out what goes on down there. It'll just be like being back at college. Call it engineering research, if you like. All you have to do is stick your hand down through the weed hatch and fiddle around with the propeller until you remove whatever it is. It'll be something simple like a plastic bag,' he reassured.

'You've got to be joking!' his son replied, recoiling from the area.

'It's just a bit of cold water. You're only going to put your hand in it. You'll be fine.'

The young man looked at his mother and shook his head. 'No way am I sticking my hand in that,' he protested and walked away, red faced and clearly upset.

Mr Captain arranged his now-muddied hat squarely on his head and addressed his wife who, to be frank, was on the side of her son. She was about to say, 'You wouldn't catch me putting my hand in it either,' when her husband let forth.

'What have we brought up, a bloody wimp? All that money on private education and he's afraid to put his hand in a bit of cold water. He should bloody well grow up!' he shouted, as he lifted the metal hatch that covered the engine.

He coughed loudly as an overwhelming cloud of hot oil fumes was released into the atmosphere and, as if it would make an improvement, he waved his hand across his face. Still muttering, he took a deep breath and clambered down into the confines of the engine compartment. Being somewhat overweight, it was difficult for him to avoid snagging his clothing on the various bits of machinery and he had to tuck himself in as he made his way down below. He finally squeezed into the tight corner at the stern, carefully avoiding the still-hot exhaust pipe.

'Oh no, no, no,' he advised himself, whilst pointing at the scalding engine.

Crouching between the fuel tanks, he found the large steel wing-nut that secured a watertight panel. This allowed access to the propeller without the need to go over the side into the canal and get wet.

When he was finally in position and ready to lift open the weed-hatch panel, he shouted instructions to his wife. 'If we shut off the light from behind me, it makes it easier to see what's going on with the propeller. When I give the word, gently close the engine cover, but stay close in case I want it lifting open again.' His wife nodded and he poised over the weed hatch. 'OK, go ahead...close the cover.'

As instructed, she grasped the handle of the heavy metal cover but, being wet, it slipped from her hand and hit the steel deck with a bang. Turning an ear in the direction of the engine compartment, she enquired, 'You OK?' She listened intently but there was no understandable reply. 'Just the usual swearing,' she thought.

Job done and smiling, she stepped off the boat clutching a fresh mug of hot tea. She watched the steam rise in the chilly air and thought about the changing seasons. Then, from the corner of her eye, she became aware of something curious happening. Her gaze was drawn to the canal water at the rear of the boat. Swirls of crimson were mixing with the brown canal water and turning it into a murky red.

She trembled, dropped the cup and shouted to her son. 'Get off the boat now!'

Her son, who was unaware of the circumstances, casually walked down the passageway, phone in hand. 'Say something?' he asked coolly.

'Get off now!' his mother repeated, but louder.

'Why?'

'Don't ask, just get off!'

Meanwhile, down below in the engine compartment, her husband struggled on. He was finding it difficult; his ears were ringing and now his breathing was becoming laboured from the fumes. 'Bleeding wimp, he should be doing this. If only he would get off his arse and grow up,' he grumbled.

He felt his way in the darkness, totally unaware of what was happening on the other side of the steel hull. With a grunt, he lifted out the heavy weed-hatch panel, paused to steady himself, then plunged his hand through the opening into the canal water. He was feeling around the propeller for items such as plastic bags or old electrical wire, items that usually fouled the blades, but instead he felt what seemed like a clump of earth covered in grass. It felt slimy and he couldn't get hold of it, so he decided to have a look. He leaned over as best he could and peered down the weed hatch.

The battered remains of a severed human head appeared to stare back at him through the swirls of canal water.

The captain lurched back, grabbing the still-hot exhaust for support then banging his head on the steel cover. He screamed for his wife to open the hatch but she was on the embankment, shielding her son's eyes from what she believed had been a terrible accident.

In his frantic efforts to flee the situation, Mr Captain shredded his clothing and lacerated his legs on the razor-sharp components that hindered his escape. Eventually he was able to put his back against the heavy engine cover and heave it open. With his head and shoulders above the deck, he held up his burnt, gore-covered hands and wailed for help.

***

'Just a head, nothing else?' said Inspector Digger to his colleague Sergeant Spade as they watched the distraught family, now wrapped in silver-foil blankets, being escorted away to an ambulance.

'Yes. I'm afraid we'll have to manage without fingerprints for the moment,' Spade sniggered.

It Could Happen Anywhere.

To anyone driving through the anonymous cluster of houses in the middle of nowhere that made up the village of Throttle, it would be difficult to give its history a moment's consideration, particularly on wet miserable days of which there were many. However, just like many other stone-built, coal-smoke blackened villages, appearances could be deceptive. The trials and tribulations that determine the layout and character of an inhabited area are many, and some are best kept secret.

Few of the present residents of Throttle had any inkling of what determined the hotchpotch of houses and factories that now exist. If they could be bothered to look, they would have found information about the main contributory factor in the dusty archives of the town hall. It showed that the people of Throttle had experienced an economic rollercoaster for as long as anyone could remember; it was no wonder that some residents had inherited a bitter, cynical outlook on life even though they could not understand why.

The financial ups and downs had mostly, but not entirely, been connected to the existence of an enormous stone-built mill that used to be situated in the centre of the village. It dominated the area and cast dark shadows over the terraced streets. Some residents blamed its very existence for the bouts of depression that affected the locals; they were sad before SAD was invented. Others were more positive. During the wool-spinning era, almost all of the villagers worked there. The income was greatly appreciated and so, to preserve their meagre standard of living, jobs were surreptitiously handed down the family line. As families expanded, more terraced houses had to be built to accommodate them; as a consequence, shops and other services thrived and the community's wealth increased.

Then fortunes changed. With the decline of the wool business many mills, which had once boasted that they clothed the world, stood silent. The mill in Throttle was not immune to this and, with the owner being unable to diversify, bankruptcy came to pass. The massive mill closed and, as a result, the district fell on hard times again.

Exposure to decades of inclement weather took its toll on the ill-maintained mill and the structure started to fall into disrepair until forward-thinking Alfred Bullock purchased the crumbling wreck and saved it, just before the bulldozers moved in. The deal was financed by what he could sell off as scrap so, in effect, the mill cost him nothing. His plan was to turn it into self-contained units that anyone could afford to rent; in turn, the tenants would employ other locals so jobs would become plentiful once more.

This project ran successfully for a number of years until an accident forced Mr Bullock into premature retirement. He misguidedly passed on the running of the company to his son, Roland. Unfortunately Roland did not possess his father's business acumen and the mismanagement of the enterprise led to financial ruin. Burdened with considerable debt, Roland felt he had no option other than to demolish the mill and put the land up for housing development.

In the short term this was bad news for Throttle, until a major new link road was constructed that connected with the major arterial roads and motorways in the area. Employees could now commute from Throttle to work elsewhere, so employment and fortunes began to improve once more. In addition, a chemical manufacturing company moved in and utilised a small mill on the outskirts town. If cubic meters of steam belching into the atmosphere could be related to profit, it would appear that it was very successful. This also helped the employment prospects for the town's residents and, on the back of this upturn in their fortunes, many of the chemical factory employees saddled themselves with considerable mortgages and debt. They never thought that such a large company could get into difficulties... could it?

The day before the boat incident ... other casualties

Another beneficiary of the town's recent prosperity was The Crown, a stone-built pub complete with flagged floors, leaded windows and roaring fires. It was originally named after a monarch, but no one could remember which one. A regular, who was asked if *he* knew which monarch the pub was named after, sought inspiration for his answer from the array of overweight drinkers with protruding beer bellies and replied, 'Henry the Eighth?'

Now deemed to be the hub of the community, The Crown served good food at the right price and had a decent range of real ale, much to the delight of beer connoisseurs. But not everyone was happy; those living close by endured the endless noise of drunks, late-night taxis and the sight of empty beer casks blocking the pavement.

The landlord sympathised and attempted to put matters right, but he was also quoted as saying, 'Get real. If you live next to a pub what do you expect?'

The busiest period was Friday lunchtime; the addictive aroma of meat pie and mushy peas laced with pickled beetroot being hastily ferried from the kitchen created a feeding frenzy that customers queuing for beer could not resist. The shift changeover at the local factory was the reason for the hectic period; some workers had a quick pie and a pint before the afternoon shift, others quenched their thirst having just finished an early shift.

Today, despite the intense heat from the roaring fire, some workers were feeling a cold draught. One man felt it necessary to explain the reason for his inebriated condition. 'I've worked there for twenty years and all you get is a paltry ten grand,' said the former worker, having just been made redundant from the chemical factory. He was waving a brown envelope whilst leaning on the bar, one arm supporting a dripping pint glass and the envelope, the other arm leaning on a damp beer towel.

The other customers knew him and were sympathetic to his circumstances but surprised by his behaviour. He had also caught the attention of the landlord, who was eager to maintain a sociable atmosphere in the establishment, so reached out to him and offered advice. 'Don't go flashing that about, you'll get robbed or lose it or something. Put it away or go stick it in the bank.'

The man turned sharply and slopped more beer on the bar. There was a pause before he steadied himself, took a large intake of breath and replied, 'In the bank? In the bank? Those bastards will rip you off as soon as look at you,' he shouted.

The landlord was getting more and more annoyed with the performance and was about to confront him when, with tears in his eyes, his customer spelt out his predicament. 'I'm fifty-five so I've got ten years before I can claim my pension. The likelihood of me getting another job at fifty-five is next to frigging zero, so I've got ten grand to last me ten years. Do you know what that works out at? Well, do you?'

The drunk stared at the others in the room, waiting for an answer. The landlord, who was fairly competent at mental arithmetic, knew the answer but still shook his head.

'Well, I'll tell you...twenty quid a week.' The man turned to the other customers and raised his voice. 'Twenty quid a week. How far do you think that will go?'

The landlord shook his head again. He was in a dilemma: he felt for the man but the chap was ruining the lunchtime mood. Beer had stopped being served and the pies were either getting cold or burning in the oven. There were others who were sitting on manila envelopes, some staring glumly into their beer, the rest just staring into space.

The room stood momentarily silent. A barmaid held a beer glass under a pump but did not pull the handle. The landlord edged forward but stopped as the drunk took a swig from his glass and, with beer dripping from his chin, started again. 'It's a bleeding disgrace... Do you know what they're doing? Well, I'll tell you. This factory has been here since soap an' stuff were invented, and now they're farming it out to be made abroad. Apparently they can get it made near half the price in India. Do you know the workers out there sleep alongside the machines at night in case somebody nicks their job? It's right...I've seen it on the telly. We had a union once, we even had a shop steward. Not seen him for ages, don't know what's happened to him. He would have sorted the bastards out, but these days everyone thinks they can look after themselves. They don't want a union, so we've become weak... Well, look where it's got you, you – set of scabs!' he shouted across the room to a set of workers huddled in a corner who had been told their jobs were precarious but safe.

The landlord had had enough; he walked out from behind the bar and confronted the irate individual. 'Calm down, for goodness' sake. I'm going to have to ask you to leave if you don't tone it down a bit.'

'It's OK, I'm going anyway. I wouldn't be seen drinking with this pile of scum,' the man shouted loudly enough for the entire pub to hear.

He ripped open the envelope, peeled off a note that was far in excess of the bill and threw it onto the beer-soaked bar. 'Here, keep the bleeding change,' he grumbled, stuffing the envelope in his back pocket.

As he made his way across the room, silence followed until he closed the door. There was a pause as people reflected on his predicament, but within minutes normal service resumed. The sound of chatter reached its usual volume and they forgot him.

The company had kept the redundancy plans secret until the very last moment that the shift had ended in order to prevent any trouble, so the shock of the announcement had yet to sink in. Two other workers who had been made redundant remained silent, deep in their own thoughts. They had worked alongside each other for many years and were not afraid to voice their opinions or seek a colleague's point of view.

Derek, who had worked at the factory since leaving school, had never been in this situation before and was short on ideas for the future. He broke the silence. 'What am I going to do on Monday? What are you going to do, Geoff?' he asked.

'Don't rightly know,' Geoff replied. 'I could eke it out till summat crops up but I've a lot longer to go than him and, as he said, it won't last that long. If you put it in the bank there's bugger-all interest. Can't live off that.' A momentary pause gave him time to speculate. He was searching for a positive. 'There's no jobs round here, none that I can do, but I'll have to find summat. I suppose I could buy a franchise. I always fancied a franchise but never needed one, or could afford one till now.' He shrugged his shoulders as if to say, 'The options are limited.'

Derek felt lost and so decided to hang on to Geoff's shirt-tail. 'What's a franchise?'

Geoff smiled at him. 'It's where you buy into a business and then run it as your own.'

'What...like a shop?'

'No, it's like providing a service – oven cleaning, dustbin cleaning, things like that. There are loads. There's even a monthly magazine and it's full of them.'

Derek mulled over the limited detail then gave his reply. 'So let me get this right. You put your money in and then they give you a brush, a ten-grand brush. Well, stuff that.'

'No it's not like that. You get a mop and bucket as well.'

They struggled to laugh, then drank up and went outside.

'Seems weird not going to the factory, not bumping into mates in the canteen. Any way...see you around,' Derek said.

'Yes, see you. Take care of yourself,' Geoff replied.

As Derek disappeared from view, Geoff furtively got out his mobile and his wallet. Reading from a tatty business card, he dialled a number he had hoped he would never need.

The phone was answered immediately. 'George Bulman,' a voice answered.

'Looks like I'm in a position to take up your offer,' Geoff said with a trace of resignation.

The man on the other end could hardly contain his excitement. 'Hey that's really good, really good. You'll not regret it. Where are you?'

'I'm just outside The Crown. Why?'

'Excellent. I can meet you in the cafe just down the road. Ten minutes and we can seal the deal there and then.'

'Oh... OK,' replied Geoff, shocked at the urgency.

He stood motionless. He had been up a long time; his shift had started at 6am and now, eight hours later, he was outside the pub, sacked from his job and already he had said yes to a man he hardly knew. A shudder ran down his spine and the hair prickled on the back of his head. 'Can this be true? I'm not dreaming, am I?'

Meanwhile, still in the pub and clutching an envelope, another redundant worker was getting advice from his mates.

'We're off to Florida. Why don't you come with us? We'll have a real laugh. We went there last year.'

Across the table, a more sober colleague added a word of caution. 'Oh aye, a real laugh. 24/7 gambling, there's gambling everywhere. Do you know that if you go for a pee there are machines at eye level? In the time it takes to have a squirt, you can lose fifty quid. Last year one bloke blew all his money in three days. Spent the rest of the time in his room. He ended up cadging off us to buy a burger – he was well pissed off.'

The encouragement went round the table.

'You'll be fine. You've just got to keep a rein on it. We broke even last year. The guy who blew it all panicked when he began to lose. He started to put bigger and bigger amounts on to get back what he'd lost and, before he knew it, it had all gone. But that was because he couldn't control himself. You wouldn't be like that, would you?'

The man stared across the table and decided he'd heard enough. He stood up, folded the envelope and stuffed it deep in his pocket.

'Er no, I would hope not. But I'm going to pass on the trip, if you don't mind. Don't think it's my kind of thing. I'll see you around.'

A very brief encounter

As arranged, Geoff met George Bulman in the café. It was a short meeting, shorter than he would have liked, but what transpired was that within minutes he was ten grand lighter and had only a promise to show for it. As he walked home, he wondered how he would be able to convince his wife that his plan was OK and would provide an income. The issue that most concerned him was the fact that this venture was not exactly legal. 'But beggars can't be choosers,' was his reasoning.

He had hardly set foot in the house before the interrogation and the argument started.

'Oh, Ange, don't be like that.'

But Ange was, and loud. 'Gone! Ten grand gone! Are you mad? Did you just give it away? Gullible – not half! They really saw you coming. You gave it to a complete stranger! Did you have mug written on your forehead?'

On several occasions Geoff opened his mouth to speak but he could not get a word in.

'So you will be servicing these machines, will you? Where does the money come from?'

'I'll be working with this bloke. He gives me the contacts and tells me which machines to service.'

'What's he called? Where does he live? Why have you not mentioned him before?

'He's called George. Look, trust me. He seems OK… OK?'

Ange was not convinced and started to talk in a much louder voice. 'Fine. It's just that you've only had the money in your hand for a matter of hours and already this "George" has come out of the woodwork and taken it all off you. And "seems OK" is not a phrase that gives me confidence. Go get the money back. If he is OK, like you say, there will not be an issue. Have you got a contract or a receipt, anything that says what you've paid and the likelihood you have of earning a living?'

'Well, er, no, not at the moment. I'll speak to him, see what he can do.'

'You are a bloody fool. First chance we get to have something for a rainy day and you blow it. Well, in the morning you and I are going to find this George the Robber and sort him out. We'll take my brother Arthur, he's a big bloke and he won't mess about. I can't believe it – ten grand! You've not had it for more than twenty-four hours. That could have got us a nice holiday or a new kitchen. A proper car, for God's sake, better than that wreck outside. What's his surname?'

Geoff wandered into the kitchen. He realised that what he had done was rash but he was under pressure. He switched on the kettle and let Ange's voice drift away. He was starting to believe her words and his eyes filled up; reaching for the coffee mugs, he noticed a tremor in his hand. The emotion of the day was getting to him.

'Fuck's sake, how on earth could I have been so hasty? I panicked at the thought of being out of a job. I just handed it over and then George was gone, ten grand with him. I've never held ten grand before and it slipped through my fingers like sand. Maybe I'm not capable. Maybe I am stupid,' he thought.

'Well, what have you got to say for yourself?' demanded his wife as she leaned against the door frame to the kitchen.

'Maybe I'm just stupid.'

'I'll say you are, but don't worry. We'll sort it tomorrow.'

An alternative plan

Derek couldn't sleep. He tossed and turned for hours, confused about his future – or the lack of it. He kept thinking about what he could or couldn't do. And then there was the franchise and what Geoff had said.

'And I'm still not sure what a franchise is. It sounds a bit posh for me. Maybe you have to be brainy,' he mused at the bathroom mirror.

He got dressed then realised it was only 5am. 'Soddin' hell, my body thinks I'm going to work. I'm way too early.' He sat at the kitchen table and ate toast to kill the time, but it dragged on and he got depressed. Like all the others who had been made redundant, he just had not seen it coming.

'If we'd been given some notice maybe we could have planned for it and then we wouldn't be in the situation … like we are now,' he grumbled, getting angry.

The next time he looked at the clock it was six thirty. 'Should be open by now,' he thought, as he put on his jacket.

He dashed to the paper shop and waited till the owner unlocked the door. 'Bloody hell, can you not sleep?' asked the newsagent.

Derek pushed past him. He bought the local newspaper and a heavy, glossy magazine. The newsagent smiled as he put the cash in the till. 'Plenty to keep you going there,' he smirked.

Derek smirked back but said nothing. Once outside, he opened the classified adverts in the local press and scanned the job vacancies. 'Nothing. Shit!'

He screwed up the paper and threw it in the rubbish bin then opened the magazine. It made him smile. 'That's better. It's just like Geoff said.'

He walked briskly home, keeping his finger on the page that had caught his eye. He presented it to his wife, Evelyn, who was still in her pyjamas, sitting at the table and was having her first cup of tea of the day after yet another disturbed night.

'What do you think?' he enthused.

Evelyn's expression indicated that she was not too impressed but she told him anyway. 'What do I think? I think you are bloody mad. Go and get a proper job.'

Showing his wife an advert in *Franchise Monthly*, and determined not to be put off by her comment, Derek read it out loud. 'Says here: "Be your own boss, work hours to suit yourself, with our tried and tested method the sky's the limit for your earnings."'

Evelyn had experienced this level of enthusiasm before and let fly. 'You can't even get out of bed in a morning – it's me that sets the clock – never mind being your own boss! It takes will-power and self-belief to run your own business, not to mention lots of cash up front.'

'But we have lots of cash,' he muttered.

'You are not using your redundancy money to start up a tin-pot company. How much is it, anyway?'

'Five grand down, and another five grand when you get started,' Derek muttered.

'So that's it, then. Money all gone, in one fell swoop.'

'You get lots of support and you go to meetings and meet other entrepreneurs.'

Evelyn turned on him again. 'Oh, so you're an entrepreneur now, are you? One minute you are an out-of-work soap-mould filler, the next you're an entrepreneur. Well, get you.'

'There are no other jobs for me round here. I've looked. I'm going to have to diversify. As they were handing out the envelopes, they were suggesting that everything would be alright so long as we retrain – but as what? I've just looked at the local ads and there's nothing. How do you know what to train for if the jobs are not there in the first place? I would be training to go on the dole. What's the point of that?'

'Diversify? You're full of fancy words. Where have you heard that?'

'It were on an overhead projector as we were walking out,' Derek explained. 'They kept talking about broadening your horizons. I've thought so hard about horizons, my head hurts. I'm not skilled at anything other than filling soap moulds but they've taken that away from me, so what else can I do but make use of the money?'

His wife sat on the sofa and folded her arms. 'Do what you like with the money but, if you blow it, I'll kill you.'

'Thanks, love.' He smiled but it was a sickly one.

A silent breakfast is followed by a silent car journey

Normally when Geoff and Ange went out together the banter flowed freely. On this occasion, they cranked up the old car and drove the whole way without speaking, both filled with their own thoughts about what they would say and how the meeting would play out.

Following the minimal instructions on how to get to the industrial estate was tricky. Usually Geoff drove and Ange navigated, but he refused to ask for directions and she didn't offer any guidance. Eventually they arrived at the industrial estate and cruised down row upon row of anonymous units. They nodded to each other when a unit fitted the description. After parking up, they peered through the windscreen.

Ange was still angry and offered a negative remark. 'Not many clues to this new career. No bright neon lights, no big hoarding saying your future is here. Not even a name. Funny really, that's just what I was expecting,' she sniggered.

'Try to be positive, love. Remember this guy is trying to help me out,' Geoff pleaded.

He counted the doors along the building until he spotted a rusty entrance tucked away; no number or title, and no loading bay, just a single door sheathed in steel with a large padlock dangling from an equally large chain. His heart sank.

'Needs a coat of paint. Hope this isn't an indicator of the opportunity,' he thought.

Ange hammered on the rusty door and, after what seemed like ages, it creaked open. In contrast to the ill-maintained door, George was sporting a neat white shirt and a tie; even the boiler suit he was wearing had been ironed. He smiled and welcomed them in.

'Get in,' Ange said angrily as she pushed Geoff through the door.

She did not hesitate; as soon as they were within the building, she took control 'We've come about the money, the money you've taken from our Geoffrey.'

'I'm afraid she's not convinced,' Geoff butted in apologetically from behind.

George put down his tools and wiped his hands. It was then that Geoff noticed another side to him.

'That's OK,' George said. 'How can I help you?'

'I'm not happy that you've taken my Geoffrey's redundancy money off him,' Ange retorted. 'We had plans for that. I want a new kitchen.'

'That's OK. Have it back – but it's a missed opportunity. He won't find another job around here,' George said, strolling to his office and returning with the envelope. 'It's a shame. Golden opportunity under the circumstances. Lots of others will be chasing the same jobs. This one, however, has been given to him on a plate.'

He held out the envelope then stood nonchalantly, hands in pockets, whilst Ange went on 'That's as maybe, but he's only had the money ten minutes and he's handed it over to a stranger.'

'Sometimes these things are meant to be,' George stated calmly.

Geoff could feel the opportunity slipping through his fingers just like the cash the previous day.

The two men watched as Ange gazed around, looking at the many types of vending machine, all apparently stripped down, neatly arranged and supposedly requiring maintenance. Deep inside, she was impressed by the organised, tidy nature of the workshop, not to mention George's demeanour and slicked-back hair.

Her rant over with, she also offered another side to her personality. 'What do you do, exactly? 'she asked softly, softly enough to make Geoff's head turn.

'I repair damaged machines or alternatively upgrade them to be more secure,' George said. 'We charge the companies for the service or sell them on. They're always getting broken. It's a good living and I just thought that your man needed a chance, an opportunity to prove himself.'

'He does, but why is it so much money? It's a hell of a lot to be giving over to a stranger.'

'It's a kind of deposit. I have to know that he is trustworthy. Responsibility is a curious commodity. I cover a lot of companies, big companies, and I have to know that he can be relied upon; they have thousands tied up in these machines. And besides, if he does the job proper and follows my guidance, he should get his money back very quickly.'

George deliberated for a moment then held out his hand. 'OK, how about a half partnership for five grand? That way you get a new kitchen and he gets a new job.'

Geoffrey smiled behind his wife's back but his expression fell when he saw how much they smiled at each other.

The other side of the coin-slot

'Hey, Geoff, its Derek. You'll never guess what.' He left a message and hoped Geoff would get back to him, but he didn't.

Derek had recently returned from his first meeting at a local hotel with We Vend Everything Inc. When he'd arrived, the smartly dressed presenter introduced himself then guided him into a meeting room where other prospective candidates were sitting around a large table. A quick glance at the others made Derek swallow hard; they had laptops, pens and mobiles at the ready. One candidate had even removed his watch and placed it beside his notepad as though he was going to time the event. 'They all look so business-like and here I am, lucky to have a pen,' he thought.

'OK, good morning,' the presenter said too cheerfully. He ushered Derek to a seat then handed out pieces of thin white card. 'Can you write the name that you would like to be called on this card and place it in front of you? I'm hopeless with names.' He laughed, but no one else did.

They sat through a long-winded presentation on the history and the future of coin-slot vending. Some eagerly took notes irrespective of what the man said; others just listened. Derek felt as though he should also take notes but he couldn't think of anything to write, so he doodled, listened, made facial expressions and nodded his head, as though he was absorbing and understanding every word.

This pretence was difficult to maintain and very quickly he started to lose control. The room was warm from the sun streaming through the windows and he had a problem trying to stay awake. He did his best to remain alert but a loud, uncontrollable yawn embarrassed him. 'Sorry, sorry, didn't get much sleep last night,' he apologised.

He rearranged his seating position, sat upright and coughed to clear his throat. The presentation droned on. 'Pointless,' he thought, as the overhead screen displayed black-and-white images of early coin-slot machines.

The presenter noticed his audience's lack of enthusiasm and decided to move on. He shut down the overhead projector and opened a cardboard box containing brochures. 'I'll bet you are all waiting for the part where we talk money.'

'Finally,' one participant groaned as he reached for his calculator.

The presenter passed around glossy folders; emblazoned on the front was the image of man who, according to the smile on his face, was very pleased with himself. The caption read: *Sack your boss and be master of your own destiny...*

Derek opened his file and was confronted with statistics, graphs and, on one page, a large pie chart that indicated the market share of vending machines in comparison to products sold by retail shops. His eyes glazed over.

The presenter continued. 'This opportunity will not be anything like the traditional way of working. You will, of course, be self-employed and as such be expected to complete your own income-tax return, VAT return and pension contributions. Most of the work you do will be on the customers' premises in the evenings; so as not to upset the punters, we expect you to dress professionally. You will be required to set up an account with the company so you can order stock. You will be on hand

24/7 for any problems and stand any losses that may occur. Are there any questions?

Derek looked around. He had no questions but in the mumbling that could be heard from the others, he could make out '24/7!! Stand losses!! Tax!! VAT!!'

The presenter ignored the mumbling and carried on. 'No questions? OK, then. As you can see, this is no ordinary career opportunity. You will be handling expensive machines and valuable stock and, as a reflection of that responsibility, can I refer you to the bottom of the last page? It's five thousand pounds down and five thousand when you get started.'

The sound of indignation grew until one point of view was clearly heard. 'Stuff that!'

The presenter allowed the door to close behind those individuals who were refusing to participate in this wonderful, life-changing opportunity. Moments later, Derek was the only candidate left in the room.

The presenter approached and held out his hand. 'Welcome to the company. You and I are going to make some awesome money and have fun doing it. Are you ready, er...?' The presenter looked down at the card. 'Er, Derek.'

Derek began to sweat. Prior to this moment, he had been drifting away and the information had passed him by. He looked at his blank notebook then tentatively opened the folder. 'Could you go through that again?'

A new case, same old problem

Not far from the village of Throttle a much larger town, now deemed to be a city, contained a building that any crystal-ball gazing architect would have shied away from. Fifty years earlier the police station was a state-of-the-art, modern, minimalistic structure that the employees were proud to enter. Now the featureless concrete construction was mocked as a carbuncle wedged between the classic Victorian grandeur of the town hall and the central library. It was suggested that the building should be demolished before it fell down, but lack of funding had prevented any rebuilding programme.

Inspector Digger and Sergeant Spade sat in their bland, uninspiring office; they were each reading the back page of a tabloid newspaper and were idly bemoaning the England football, rugby and crickets teams' inability to win anything.

Digger held court. 'They are hopeless! These people are paid thousands a week and they can't kick, pass or catch a ball. If it were up to me, they would be fined a thousand pounds every time they miss the goal or drop a catch. They'd soon buck their ideas up.'

They were nodding in agreement about the depressing sporting situation when a shadow appeared at the frosted-glass door. It was the unmistakable contour of their boss.

'By your beds!' hissed Digger militarily.

The door opened smartly and their superior officer, Chief Inspector Peacock, stood in the door frame. His wide, wild eyes followed the walls, floor and ceiling. He remained on the threshold, as though afraid he might catch something if he entered. His facial expression signified disgust. 'Ah...D and S, glad I've caught you in. Point is, why aren't you out detectering?'

'Good morning, sir,' Digger said politely. 'We were just pondering the recent happenings in Throttle. We've decided to start the investigation prior to getting the autopsy results or any other information that could confirm the identity of the deceased.'

'From now on, do your pondering out in the field or where ever it is you operate. Upstairs is expecting results and soon. Get it?'

They nodded and looked towards the ceiling as Peacock slammed the flimsy door with almost enough force to break the glass.

They allowed his shadow to fade from view, exhaled audibly, smiled and then pointed to the kettle. As Spade organised a mid-morning brew, Digger emptied the progress file which contained one item of information: the photograph of the severed head.

'Not while we are having tea and biscuits,' Spade said. 'It'll send the milk off. Put it away.'

Digger, being the superior officer, asserted his authority. 'It's all we have and it's meant to be on the evidence board. I don't like walking near it either, gives me the creeps. Compromise – we keep it in the envelope but put it on the board.'

'Deal.' Mid-pour of the boiling water, Spade put down the kettle and looked again at the picture of the head. 'I'm not an expert but, looking at its condition, how long would you say, that it's been in the water?'

'Months.'

'That's what I would have thought, but there's been no missing persons, no murders in Throttle or the surrounding area. Something fishy going on here.'

'Hey, I like it! Fishy, canal – how did you work that into the conversation?'

'It comes naturally,' boasted Spade, touching his lapel.

They savoured the chocolate-coated digestives then Digger took charge again. 'Got to start somewhere. How about a nice smelly chemical factory? Apparently, there was a near riot there the other day, fisticuffs between the workers. Some were made redundant, some not, and you never know – someone could have a grudge. And we know what grudges mean!'

'It's fine by me,' Spade said. 'But what exactly does a chemical factory make, besides the obvious? I mean besides chemicals?'

'Not sure. Do they take chemicals and turn them into other, better, more expensive chemicals?'

They wiped away the crumbs then Spade shielded his eyes as he put the photograph of the head back in its envelope. 'That's enough for one day.'

***

Driving in their beat-up unmarked car, they arrived at the factory gate. All was revealed relating to the products made at the plant when Spade read from the hoarding. 'It seems to be mainly heavy-duty cleaning products: soap, drain and oven cleaners, that kind of thing.'

They drove into the company car park then stood back and peered up at the façade of the building. The stone structure, with its stained-glass windows, was black on one side; it was not so black on the other side. 'The prevailing wind blowing the smoke from coal fires,' observed Spade, pointing at the contrast.

As they walked up the well-worn steps, Digger stopped. 'We are being watched,' he said, nodding towards a small window where a bespectacled face was looking out.

Once up the stone steps, Spade ran a finger over the brass plaque next to the main entrance. It had been cleaned so often that it was hard to discern the inscription on it. 'Less cleaning of the plaque, more cleaning of the building. Just an observation,' he mumbled.

Inside the gloomy, heavily tiled reception area, Digger knocked on the dark, oak-framed office window and eventually a secretary slid back a small panel. 'Have you got an appointment?' she asked, peering over her glasses.

'Ah, bespectacled lady, no,' replied Digger.

Before he could get out his identification card, the secretary laid it on the line. 'Nobody will see you without an appointment. And if it's a job you're after, we have just had a round of redundancies so you won't get seen at all. I wouldn't waste your time – there's no point even filling in an application form.'

Digger stepped back and turned to Spade. 'Let me know when she's done, will you?'

'Yes, sir, Inspector Digger, sir, from the County Police Department. I will let you know when the lady has finished, sir.' Spade said it loudly enough for the entire factory to hear.

'Why didn't you say?' the secretary demanded.

'Why didn't you ask?' Spade retorted.

'OK let's start again,' Digger said. 'We are here to enquire about the circumstances leading up to the remains of a body being found in the canal not far from here.'

The lady remained silent.

'Sources have told us that last week there were almost riots here, and that threats of violence were made against certain parties. Did you witness anything? Anything out of the ordinary?'

'Afraid I don't get involved with people on the shop floor,' the secretary sniffed. 'And it's not my position to comment. But feel free to have a look round.'

'Is anyone from the management available?' Digger demanded.

'I wish I could help but they've gone on a jolly to a spa. It's a treat from the boss, who seems pleased at how they handled the round of redundancies. A bloody nerve, if you ask me.'

'Me as well,' Digger agreed. 'OK, we'll have a look around.'

'That's fine but be very careful. There are some very nasty chemicals in there – don't breathe in any fumes, tread in any puddles or touch anything, or you'll be lucky to get out in one piece.'

The small window snapped shut.

'A solemn, kind of terminal noise, wouldn't you say?' Spade said. Standing in the dim reception area, he went over the advice again. 'So … no touching, no breathing, no putting your foot in it,' he added.

Treading carefully, they went back out and around the building towards a large door that they presumed was the factory entrance.

'Crikey are you sure about this?' cautioned Spade, as he pushed at the door with a piece of wood.

They crept stealthily along an undulating cobbled entry into a dimly lit narrow warehouse; the acidic stench hit them immediately. 'Good God,' exclaimed Spade holding his hand over his mouth.

'Just a quick look. We'll see if we can speak to at least one person then it's not been a wasted journey.'

Digger wandered over to a tatty notice hanging from a hook next to a large tank. After a few seconds' reading, he exhaled loudly. 'Good Jesus, there are some seriously dangerous chemicals in here. This one, caustic soda, it says it dissolves animal fat so it can be used for soap making.'

'Really?'

'Listen to this: "Understand the dangers of caustic soda chemical. It **will** burn your skin upon contact. Do **not** let this chemical touch you in any way. Be sure to wear protective clothing. In order to avoid any contact with caustic soda, or any other harmful substance, wear rubber gloves, goggles and extremely thick rubber outerwear."' Digger looked at Spade. 'Are you thinking what I am thinking?'

Looking around for a process worker, they headed further on to where they could hear the clank of machinery. A rhythmic squeak alerted them to the approach of a scruffily dressed man wheeling a sack truck. In the gloom, the man hesitated as he got close to the detectives.

'Excuse me, can I have a word?' Digger asked.

The man stood to attention and nearly saluted. 'Yes sir.'

'This chemical, the one this notice relates to.'

The worker acknowledged the question by nodding and looking up at the notice.

'Sounds like its nasty stuff,' Digger said, with a hollow laugh.

'Caustic soda – don't go fucking about with that 'cos it will reduce you to a sticky slop as soon as you touch it.'

'Yes, only we are a bit confused. This chemical, where is it stored? If it's this dangerous, shouldn't it be locked away?'

The man grinned, exposing his need to see a dentist immediately. 'You are looking at it,' he slurred.

They turned, backed away and winced as they looked up at the huge grime-encrusted tank. 'Get cleaned regularly, does it?' Spade asked.

'Never been cleaned while I've worked here,' the worker said. 'Too expensive and dangerous. They'd have to stop production, and where would you store the stuff till you'd cleaned the tank?

'I see. Does it have a hatch, a manhole, on top?' Spade demanded.

'Why?'

'So you can see how full it is.'

'I think so, but nobody goes up there. Thank fuck we don't have to. We can tell the level from this sight glass.' The man pointed to a long, dusty, glass window situated on the side of the tank. The detectives peered at it.

'Is it always this murky?' Digger asked.

'You'd have to ask the chemist.'

'Who's he?'

'He's the manager, the one whose gone missing,' the worker said with a leer.

'Missing, missing where?'

The man looked up at the tank, sniggered and started to laugh, then he continued pushing his squeaking truck through the warehouse.

Digger looked a Spade. 'Oh, just one other thing?' he shouted to the man just before he got out of earshot. 'Has anyone else gone missing?'

'Anyone who steps out of line, it seems,' the man replied. Hollow, spooky laughter echoed through the factory space and diminished as he went around the corner.

'This place gives me the creeps, and I don't think we should stand so close to this frigging tank. Coffee time?' Digger asked.

Avoiding puddles, and not touching anything, they made their escape to a safer place in order to compare notes. The new – and only – cafe in town was busy with individuals reading the free newspapers or gawping at their mobile phones. Spade and Digger settled into the leather chairs and relaxed.

After ordering lattes and brownies, Digger leaned forward on the small round table and tried to make sense of the last few minutes. 'This is weird. People go missing and no one seems to care. And as for that factory... What happened to health and safety?'

'This is Throttle: backward, in the Dark Ages and in the middle of nowhere,' replied Spade, laughing quietly.

As Digger pondered that last statement, he notice a man hastily exiting through the door. In so doing, the man elbowed past customers who were trying to get in. Seconds later, he ran past the window. He turned, caught Digger's eye and in an instant was gone.

'Place is full of nutters,' Digger said as the coffee arrived.

'Got to be the fumes from that factory,' Spade said. 'It must send them all crackers. If the stuff in the tank dissolves your flesh, then what do the fumes do to your brain when you breathe them in?'

They arranged the cups on the table and savoured the aroma of fresh Columbian.

'Shall I be mother?' asked Spade.

'If it suits,' replied Digger. As he picked up the milk jug, a scrap of paper stuck to the base that he'd thought was the bill floated down to the table. He retrieved it and read out the message scrawled in pencil: *Check out the missing shop steward.*

He held the paper towards Spade at the same moment that a waitress walked by. 'Excuse me, have you any idea who left this note?' Digger asked, holding it up for her to read.

'Well it certainly wasn't me. Mind you, people do send messages across the cafe, but usually it's to the opposite sex asking for a date. Got a liking for shop stewards, have you?' She left him with the proper bill and gave him an exaggerated wink.

'I think you've trapped there,' laughed Spade, as he analysed the note. 'So, the scribble is hardly intelligible – that would indicate a person of low intelligence. The use of a 2B pencil suggests low income, probably manual worker or labourer.'

'Well done, Spade,' Digger said. 'So after the coffee, it's back to the mill – from a very safe distance, of course.'

'Really? Haven't we had enough for one day?'

As they left, the waitress nodded towards them and giggled to a colleague. She stopped short of pointing but it was obvious she was having a joke at their expense. Digger stopped momentarily then thought better of it.

Spade had also spotted the waitress's action and offered a thought. 'Mixed messages, not easy to discern. Was she admiring you or mocking you?'

'I'd like to think that she has respect for my uniform, even if it isn't a uniform – if you get my drift.'

Still smarting at the waitress's laughter, they set off for the mill. 'Nasty piece of work, that. Obviously she's not been on the customer-care course,' Digger said.

'Calm down,' Spade soothed. 'She's a monkey and probably gets paid peanuts. It's the only entertainment she gets all day.'

They parked up at the entrance to the mill and found the main gates closed and locked.

'What time is it?' Digger asked. 'Gone home already?'

Spade looked at his watch. 'It is coming up to five o'clock. Didn't think they would close so early.'

They got out of the car and walked up to the massive ornate gates. 'I bet steel was cheap when these were made,' Spade joked, as he admired the wrought-iron work. Peering through a gap in the gate, he spotted an old car parked next to a side entrance. 'Ah… we are not alone.'

They followed the stone wall with its barbed-wire fence on top until they arrived at yet another heavily chained gate. Spade inspected the lock then let it drop. 'Security is high on their agenda here. Take all week to pick that,' he muttered.

Digger smiled. 'See that door over there? Well, there's somebody behind it. Let's see if we can rouse them. And, as there is more than one way skin a wotsit, how's your aim?'

'Pardon?'

'Your aim, how's your aim? Be a good test this. You know the phrase "couldn't hit a barn door"? Well, all you have to do is hit that door over there and see if we can wake the sleeping giant, or whoever it is that's inside.'

'Piece of cake. Watch this,' said Spade. He selected a smooth oval stone from the gravel path, held out his arm, squinted and let fly. The stone fell yards short of the doorway.

'Piece of cake? Really? That was a clog out! Just watch this,' smirked Digger. His action was that of a fast bowler and the stone was a half brick; it spun through the air, then hit the door with a loud bang. 'See, you never lose it. I used to play for the school team and batsmen were frightened to death when I came up to the crease.'

'Let me have another go. I have to get my eye in,' suggested Spade. He selected another stone, a bit bigger this time. 'The previous was a bit to the left, so I'll adjust my feet. Here we go.'

The stone flew through the air and headed straight for the door; it would have hit it, had it not opened. The man who was leaving saw the missile and slammed the door shut just in time. Then he opened it again and rushed out holding a large hammer. 'If I catch you, I'll knock your bloody head in,' he screamed as he ran towards them.

By the time he reached the gate he was out of breath and could hardly speak.

Digger and Spade held out their IDs. 'Calm down. It was the only way we could get your attention,' Spade said. 'Now, let us in so that we can have a chat.'

'Who the hell are you?' the man choked, still trying to get his breath back.

'The police and we ask the questions.'

'Oh.'

'We are investigating the unfortunate death of somebody, and we don't know who,' Digger explained. 'And we don't know why, either. But we thought we would start here and we'd like a word, so let us in.'

The man nodded, unlocked the gate and they all walked towards the mill. By the time they reached the door, the anger had dissipated from his face and he was breathing normally. 'Now look, I've a job to finish or there'll not be any production tomorrow so I can't talk for long. I've a guard to put back on a machine and a repair to do.'

'Bit last minute for repairs, isn't it?' Spade asked.

'It's like this every day. Every day there's repairs and breakages. It's political.'

'Political? Here?'

'There's two factions who work here. On the one hand, there are the idiots who take off the guards so they can produce more units; then there's the other idiots who break the machines to slow down the production of units. I tell you, it's like working in a nut house.'

'What's a unit?' asked Spade.

'A unit is a box of five hundred bars of soap, or a box of twenty tins of cleaner, or a pack of a hundred scourers. It's bottles of strong drain cleaner this week. It's how the men get paid: over a certain number of units produced, they get a bonus. They need the bonus to get a living wage.'

'So why would anyone want to slow production down?' Digger demanded.

'Ah, well, if they can prove that only so many units were achievable on a particular day, let's say because of a machine breaking down, then the company lowers the production threshold so they still get the bonus. So you see – some want it faster, some want it slower.'

'How do they slow down production?'

'By putting a spanner in a gearwheel, or they'll cut through drive belts, or fuse the electrics… It goes on all the time. Luddites, the bleeding lot of them. I'm here every bleeding night putting stuff right for the following shifts.'

'So how do you feel having to mend what is effectively sabotage?'

'I'm in the middle of it all. I can't go to the pub in case I meet one of them saboteurs. I've had enough. The workers say I'm not maintaining the machines enough so they break down. I say I am, and it's them that's doing the damage. The management don't know who to believe, so I'm in the middle and in the bad books. No wonder there's threats that they're taking the production abroad.'

'There have been redundancies. What about them?' Spade asked.

'They were all handpicked trouble makers, from what I can see.'

'What happened to the shop steward?'

'We don't know. He had a right falling out with the management. He said that he would bring the whole workforce out on strike if the threshold weren't lowered further.'

'So what happened?' Spade persisted.

'Nobody knows. He just left. Here one day, gone the next... There's all sorts of rumours. Some say he was paid off and some say he was threatened.'

'And the chemist-stroke-manager, where's he?' Digger asked.

'He went missing the same day as the shop steward. Some say they were both paid off. Others think it's a bit more sinister.'

'Oh?'

'The owner, Mr Granville, didn't like the pair of them.'

The maintenance man picked up his hammer and was about to walk away when Spade held his arm. 'Just one more thing. I know you have to get back, but what about the stuff in the tank?'

'Oh that... Good God, steer clear of that. Don't ever walk in the puddles in that room.'

'Has there ever been any talk about people going missing that are – you know – now inside the tank.

'News to me,' the maintenance man said. 'You would have to get a body up that ladder and more than likely you would end up covered in the chemical yourself. And once it's on you, it's goodnight Vienna. It just eats away at you.'

'Yes, it seems a tall order getting a body up the ladder,' Digger said thoughtfully.

'But you could get the stuff to the body – laterally thinking.' Spade tapped his nose.

'Even that seems fraught with problems. Splashes and things.'

'But if other people are used to seeing you with a rubber suit, goggles and such, it wouldn't be that fraught, would it?' Spade surmised.

They left to let the man get on with his work.

'Did you see that he never smiled once?' Spade asked. 'He is on the edge. Did you see the way he gripped that hammer? His knuckles were white … and it's this place that has caused it. I wonder how many others are in the same boat? Seems a horrible place to work in, practically and emotionally.'

'Very astute,' replied Digger.

They walked out of the building and across the yard towards the gate. Spade turned to face the factory and then picked up a large stone. 'I reckon that, with a bit of practice, I could hit the latch on that door, no problem.'

'Put it down. You'll have him running out again and this time he might not be so calm. Luddites – long time since I've heard that word,' mused Digger, as they climbed into the car.

'I think the word originated not far from here. "Smash the frames". I remember seeing it on telly,' Spade informed him.

'What?'

'"Smash the frames", it's what the Luddites used to say. "Smash the spinning frames".'

'What?' Digger asked again.

'When the bosses introduced mechanisation, the mills could produce far more than doing it by hand. The workers' wages were dropped, so they used to say, "In that case, smash the frames." It was their way of trying to restore what they'd had before. There were riots and they had to get the police and army in.'

'So it's not just something you've seen on telly.'

'No, it's real history,' Spade said proudly.

'History *is* real, you pudding.'

'What goes around comes around. No wonder they're shipping production abroad.'

The tuition begins

The mood had settled down between Geoff and Ange and, after the initial meeting, she had warmed to the arrangement. She had even gone and bought him a new boiler suit from the market but he refused to wear it on the first day of work; he said it made him look like a rookie new boy.

He had been looking forward to the next meeting with 'George the Vend'. It had been Ange's idea to change the nickname from George the Robber to George the Vend. She said he seemed like a nice man.

'But 10pm, it's dark for God's sake! Why so late?' he muttered as he drove into the industrial estate. He had arrived early just in case he couldn't find the entrance and, despite being there only days before, the lack of signs and door numbers was still giving him issues.

Geoff parked his car in a bay a short distance away from the unit. He thought he would have a minute to himself but a proximity detector sensed his movements and security lights immediately illuminated the whole area, indicating that there was an individual in the vicinity. 'If I don't move, they will go off again in a minute,' he said, without moving his lips.

He watched the clock on the dashboard and five minutes elapsed before the lights went out with a crackle. Still he sat there; the longer he remained in his car, the more doubt crept into his mind. He held onto the steering wheel as though it were a safety barrier. Looking up into the rear-view mirror, he tilted it until he saw himself. He shook his head in disbelief. He widened his eyes and poked the bags, then spoke to the mirror.

'Two weeks ago I was happy as Larry. Look at me now, I'm ageing fast. And another thing – and it's a bit weird – but what do I tell people when they ask where I work? "Don't know, not sure, it's just a scruffy blue door on the industrial estate on the edge of town." And what do you do? "Not sure, but unfortunately I think it's a bit iffy."'

He plucked up courage and climbed out of the car. It was cold and he could see his breath as he walked across the tarmac to the unit. He knocked on the steel-clad door. The noise seemed to echo around the whole estate and it was a while before a response came.

As he waited, his mind went into overdrive. He had been promised a session that would explain everything, a friendly chat, he thought, maybe with information in a pack. In the back of his mind though, he still had massive doubts about the legality of what he was doing; he knew it was not exactly straight, but just how bent was it?

'Am I taking advantage of someone? Taking bread out of their mouths? After all, this is somebody's livelihood. Am I going to be a thief in the night? Everything I've done in my life so far has been lawful. Will I be able to sleep at night? And what about the risk of being caught, locked up for a few quid, mixing with real criminals and slopping out?'

He hesitated and then considered the positives. 'But then again, I'm in a mess. No job and the money won't last long. So, as long as I keep it quiet, it should be OK. George does it, after all, so it can't be that bad – can it?'

The door opened. 'Come in, you're late,' George grumbled, then he turned his back and walked into the partially lit workshop.

'I was early but you don't have a name over the door,' Geoff said. 'Took me ages to find it.'

George ignored him. 'Put your coat over there,' he said, pointing to a hook on the wall.

They faced each other in the gloom. Geoff didn't know if he was supposed to stand to attention or what, so he opted for casual but alert.

'Let me explain something before we move on because I want it to be clear in your mind so there won't be any doubts. OK?' George said.

'OK,' replied Geoff, a little more formally than he was used to doing.

'This is a business – a strange business, I'll grant you, but it works. It works because I'm thorough, and I'm thorough with everything I do. The business is expanding…it's getting too big for me to handle on my own, that's why I've offered you a job. But if you don't think that you can handle my thoroughness, then we better part right now.' George stepped back a pace and waited for a response.

Geoff's gaze was elsewhere; he was looking at the many shadowboards around the walls all containing tools and equipment relating to different types of vending machines. The lathes and other machinery looked freshly cleaned and oiled and there was not a speck of dirt on the benches. Paper planners adorned the walls with code numbers and dates. 'Of course I can handle it – but I *was* early,' he smirked cockily.

'OK, then. Bet you're wondering why it's this late and this dark?'

'It had crossed my mind just a bit.'

'It's because this is the time of day that you will be working and, more than likely, this is how dark or light it will be. OK so far?'

'Yep.'

'First things first: you do exactly as I say. You do not stray from the instructions, OK?'

Geoff nodded again.

'We are in the game of selecting and emptying cash boxes. I select them and you empty them, OK? I have logged every machine within a fifty-mile radius; I know when they need emptying, where they are and where the cameras are. I also know the ones to leave alone, perhaps because they don't make enough to be worth the effort, or they are too exposed and you could be seen and at risk. That is why, when I tell you to do a particular machine, you don't do the one next to it. If it is not on your list then don't do it. Get it?'

Geoff noticed an element of menace in George's voice, so replied promptly, 'Got it.'

'OK, let's move on.' George held out his arm and pointed to an array of vending machines. 'As you can see, there are many different shapes and sizes of coin-slot machines but they all have one thing in common. What is it?' He waited for a reply but Geoff was silent. 'Good God – wake up! They all have money boxes.'

'Yes, yes, of course, I thought it was a trick question,' stuttered Geoff.

They walked past the line of machines and George pointed out the location of the money boxes. 'They are all different because they are designed by different people. Each one has a way of taking the cash and dispensing the goods and, as you can see, the cash box is in a different place for each one. What you have to do is remember where the cash boxes are.'

'What, for all of them?'

'Make notes if you wish but eventually it should all be in your head.'

Geoff walked down the line of machines again and peered into the workings, then looked back and smiled. 'That should be OK.'

'Now, I'll bet you are wondering how you get to the cash box without stripping the machines down.'

'It had crossed my mind, 'cos time will be tight.'

'Precisely. Let me explain something else: some people smash their way into the machines but we don't. We do it surgically, keyhole surgery. You know where the cash box is, so a hole adjacent will provide access.'

Geoff looked bemused. 'Drilling a hole won't be quick.'

'Stand back.' George instructed.

He approached a machine and pointed to a clock on the wall. 'OK,' he said, pointing to the cash box and then towards the casing closest to it. From his tool box he produced a small power unit that had a cutter at right angles to its body. He held it against the casing and pressed a button; there was a low-level humming and grinding noise lasting no more than ten seconds and he was in. He pushed in a scoop through the hole and retrieved all the pound coins. 'Fill your bag and away.'

Geoff looked at the neatly cut hole and smiled. George also smiled then held the power unit for Geoff to inspect. 'This will cut a hole big enough for your hand or a scoop and, so long as you keep constant pressure, it will be quick and quiet. It is extremely sharp. Each tooth on the blade is tungsten-carbide tipped and honed like a razor. It is battery powered so has a limit of three holes and then needs charging from the cigar socket in your car. Twenty minutes, and it is ready again. If you look after it, it will make you a fortune. But remember, any damage to the teeth will extend the cutting time.'

They moved to a wooden bench in front of three vending machines mounted on the wall. George handed over a plastic bag containing a coverall suit and a black rucksack. 'Dark and anonymous. For the moment, you don't wear any other outfit. These are to be left here when not in use, burned if necessary, and untraceable to you. Put it on,' he snapped.

Geoff quickly donned the suit. He smiled when he realised it was a perfect fit. 'How did you know my size?'

'Doors are six feet six inches. I guessed the distance from the top of your head to the top of the door. Remember it will be gloomy and late. You could be tired but you have to be vigilant – there could still be other people around. Do not appear furtive, do not look up at cameras, do not whistle. You have to be swift, quiet and efficient, you have to look like you are the maintenance man. So your turn, two minutes top whack; any longer and you will draw attention. If more than two minutes elapse, walk away. Got it? OK, away you go.'

Geoff braced himself and waited for the second finger on the clock to reach twelve. As it passed, he moved forward and pointed to the side of the slot machine then held the power unit against it. He looked at George.

'Get on with it, time is running out,' George hissed through his teeth.

Geoff pressed the button and the unit whizzed in his hand. He held it to the casing and pressed the button again; initially it wobbled, then he gripped it tighter and managed to stabilise the motion. Within seconds it popped through.

'You've got twenty-five seconds to empty the box,' George barked.

As Geoff shovelled the coins into the sack, the odd one dropped to the floor and rolled away.

George shook his head. 'Leave them and the machine. You're bleeding hopeless.'

'I just need a bit more practice, that's all. It's the first time I've done anything like this. Don't worry, I'll sort it.'

George did not give out any encouragement. 'Same time tomorrow. I'll have three more machines set up. If you can't do it in two minutes, that's it. Understand?'

Geoff headed for the door feeling dejected. As he stepped outside, the chill caught his breath, the security lights came on and distrust filled his mind. Driving home, he wondered if he had made the right decision. Pulling out onto the main road, he stalled the car and sweat trickled down his forehead as he struggled to restart the engine. 'It's just not me.'

He opened the front door of his house as carefully as he could but some noise was unavoidable. 'Sodding hell,' he whispered, as the door latch clicked louder than he'd expected. Creeping into the dining room, he was shocked to see his wife sitting calmly at the dining table reading the newspaper.

'Have you seen the time? It's gone midnight,' Ange said, turning over another page.

'How come you are still up? I was trying not to disturb you.'

'Aye, well, you went out without saying anything. So what were you up to?'

'I've been round to George's workshop for training.'

'For training? This time of night?'

'Yes, he said it was the only time he could spare. He's busy during the day.'

'So how did it go?' she asked.

'Not sure. Not sure if it's me, not sure I can handle it.'

Ange turned to face him. 'Hang on, we are five grand down! You've only been there two hours and already you are talking pessimistic.'

'It's all different from what I'm used to. I'm used to working with a team. It were fun working at the factory, there was a buzz with the lads. This is working on my own, all serious.'

Ange had developed a soft spot for George and was looking forward to being introduced to him in a less formal atmosphere, so she could not believe her ears when Geoff came out with excuses, excuses that could inhibit her social progress. Recognising that events she had been dreaming about most of the day could be scuppered before they even got off the ground, she unfolded her arms, leant forward and offered support. 'Is there anything I can help you with?'

'I'll be OK once I get used to the workings of the machines. Only George wants me to repair them within a certain amount time, and at the moment...I can't.'

Pleased with his response, she smiled affectionately and held out her hand. 'Come on, it's getting late and you've had a hard couple of days. You go off to bed and I'll bring you up a nice mug of tea. Do you think I'll get to meet George again? If he is this busy, maybe he will need a secretary.'

Geoff trudged up the stairs, reflecting on the last forty-eight hours. 'I am out of work, lying to my wife, becoming a crook, and only hours ago I had ten grand. Now I'm down to five and it looks like it's already spoken for. And on top of that, if I didn't know any better, I'd say Ange has taken a shine to George.'

As he reached the top step, his wife followed with the promised mug of tea. 'Not many men can say they've got a job within hours of being made redundant... My little hero.'

An involuntary movement

The narrow canal meandered on the outskirts of Throttle before turning sharply inwards to run parallel with the high street. The locals were not sure which came first, the road or the canal. Old maps indicated the canal running past the now-defunct mills; it was only a theory that the tracks used for loading and unloading the barges evolved into roads and, almost at the same time, a town was born. This fortunate diversion into the centre of town added to the use and popularity of the waterways. Walkers, cyclists and anglers all enjoyed the facility and, with the development of the narrow-boat hire companies further upstream, Throttle began to take off as a tourist attraction. Chandleries and tea shops sprang up to support the new tourist industry and, after the reinvention of the waterway maintenance department, the newly renovated lock gates got a fresh lick of paint and looked smart again.

To add to the overall charm of the waterway, the side verges of the towpath were tended and planted with wildflowers by volunteers from the Friends of the Towpath Group, whose mission was to ensure that the route remained litter free and pleasing to the eye.

One such volunteer, who had drawn the short straw of weeding the verges, rested a moment on her patented kneeler. As she stretched her stiffening back, she was alarmed to hear the sound of rushing, cascading water. Having recently returned from a trip to Niagara Falls, she was familiar with the crash of millions of gallons of water – but she was in Throttle.

She turned towards the canal and noticed water overflowing the top of the gate paddle. The reason was that the canal pound between the locks was overfull and the excess water had to go somewhere. As boats moved in and out of the locks, the water emptied into the lock pound beneath; if the pound was full, the water went round the lock via a by-wash, a drainage tunnel connecting one lock to another to feed water eventually to the canal at the bottom of the flight.

The shocked volunteer ran to the lock-keeper's office and hammered on the door. She was beginning to panic. A notice taped to the window advised that, due to financial cuts, the office would only be manned at weekends. Today was Tuesday. She felt alone and betrayed. 'So it's OK for me to work on Tuesdays,' she bawled.

The overflowing water had filled the lock and was now running over the top of the next gate paddle. It was a fifteen-foot drop down to the canal below and the sound of the water had got louder. 'It'll flood the town,' she screamed, whilst running up and down the weed-free towpath.

It was a while before the police and rescue services arrived but, as they had never dealt with anything like this before, they could only stand, watch and clear the area. A team of specialist workmen eventually arrived and discussed a plan of action. They stood in a huddle and watched the water crashing over the top of the lock at an increasing rate.

Emergencies like this did not happen that often. Although they were well informed on the theory of the lock-gate method of lifting or lowering boats up or down an incline, their day-to-day tasks usually involved floods or landslides.

An unelected chap took charge. 'I've been down to where the by-wash empties into the lock and there's nothing coming out, so it's obviously blocked. Long poles needed to unblock it – but in the meantime, is it not possible to barrage the canal further upstream?'

'What with?' was the unhelpful reply.

'About half a mile away there's a crane and a stack of wooden beams that can be lowered across the canal. They fit them in those slots in the banking and it's this kind of situation that they are provided for.'

Another member of the team dashed the theory. 'Do you know how old they are? The cranes are rusty as hell and the beams are probably rotten. They've been there for years, they're just ornaments.'

'We've got to do something! The water's flowing like crazy.'

They raced off to get long barge poles to poke down the by-wash.

'Right, OK, two men to a pole. Let's see what's going on,' the leader said.

They prodded the poles down into the flooded by-wash and confirmed that something was hindering the flow. A momentary smile that lit up the faces of the workmen on locating the problem was replaced with despair as the blockage refused to budge.

'I've hit on something, but it won't shift. Come on, get another pole in. Let's see if we can force it through.'

Three men systematically rammed long poles down the tunnel. As they worked, strangely coloured slime flowed back out of the tunnel, accompanied by flies and a puke-making smell. The men halted to regain their breath and noticed they were not alone; onlookers, who were sitting high on the embankment wall, began shouting encouragement in time with their efforts. Sweating and aching, and still unaware of what it was that they were trying to dislodge, they pressed on to the sound of, 'Go on, lads, one more time.'

'It's giving way. It feels very soft, though,' shouted one man, as his pole began to go deeper into the tunnel.

'We've done it!' shouted another, as water started to rush down the by-wash and burst into the lower lock pound.

As the water settled, the cause of the blockage became apparent. Onlookers threw up at the sight of a bloated, rotting carcase that floated, half-submerged, in the middle of the canal.

Once the source of the blockage had been identified as human remains, a more urgent response gathered pace that included the arrival of Digger and Spade. The blob, as it was referred to by the onlookers, floated unhelpfully in the middle of the canal. Heads shook as a considerate means of reaching it deserted them; grappling hooks had been dismissed as 'not the right thing to do'.

'It looks like we have found the other bit to the head,' suggested Digger.

Spade wandered across the lock gate for a better view then gave his assessment. 'It's a bit of a mess. The workmen mashed it up trying to unblock the canal. Point is, did he fall or was he pushed? Is it crime-related or just an unfortunate accident?'

At that moment a constable interrupted their debate. 'Can I have a word, sir? There's a gentleman here who sounds like he could shed some light on the situation.'

'Bloody hell...shock horror! It's a miracle,' Spade said.

The sarcasm was not lost on the constable, who held out his hand and introduced the witness to the detectives. 'This is Mr Jones, who lives just across the road. He has something to share with you.'

'Thank you, constable. Mr Jones, it's good of you to come forward.'

Usually they had to prise information out of the public, or even threaten them with prosecution, so someone coming forward of their own free will was a big surprise. Digger smiled at Spade who immediately got out his pen and pad, then said, 'Go on, then, what have you got?'

'I think I know who this is,' Jones said. 'I can tell by the colour of his boiler suit. He works at the factory – or he did. But if you want confirmation, he should have ten grand in his back pocket.'

'Ten grand? Really?' queried Spade.

'He were one of them made redundant the other day, only he were shouting his mouth off in the pub. Everybody saw him. He would have become a target – there are some ruffians in that pub. He stuffed the money in his back pocket and left, and that's the last we saw of him.'

'I see. Well, thank you very much,' Spade said. 'You have been a great help.'

Digger walked back and stood on the stone embankment; the human remains were barely buoyant and showed no signs of drifting towards the bank. 'We'll have to do something before it sinks to the bottom.' He turned to Spade, smiled, and then slowly, slightly louder than normal and just within earshot of the onlookers, said to his colleague, 'I don't know how we are going to do it but we need to search him in order to retrieve the ten grand that's in his back pocket.'

Before he could say 'only joking', six onlookers had jumped in the canal and waded towards the semi-submerged 'blob'.

A new day dawns for the entrepreneur

Derek reported back to his wife, Evelyn, that he had eventually signed the contract with We Vend Anything Inc. She reluctantly agreed that what you never had you never missed; as she hadn't set eyes on the ten grand, there was no point bemoaning its loss. So she came on board.

'I'll do the donkey work and you can do the fancy stuff, you know, like filling in the forms and such,' Derek patronised, as he picked up the sandwiches she had provided.

Evelyn blew a sigh of resignation as he stepped through the front door for his first meeting with his new boss.

Outside the town yet another industrial estate had sprung up seemingly overnight, and it was a familiar story of look at the information board at the entrance to the estate, find the name of the company and follow the numbers. The numbers went on and on and, before Derek arrived at his destination, the back of his neck was aching from looking upwards. He parked in a loading bay and knocked on a door that said 'Staff Only'.

'Well, I am staff,' he reasoned to himself.

The man from the presentation recognised him and greeted him like a long-lost relative, stopping just short of kissing his cheek. 'Welcome, welcome! Have we got a day for you? It's a whistle-stop tour today, Derek. We are going to get you all prepared for the open road to success, but first a quick tour of the building,' he gushed in an unnecessary loud voice as he handed over a white coat and a hairnet. 'Don't worry about the look of the hairnet. We all look daft in these but we have to remember that personal hygiene is our number-one priority. Don't want anyone getting hair in their chocolate, do we?'

'Er no,' said Derek.

They walked through large, floppy plastic doors to a delivery department surrounded by a mountain of cardboard boxes. The presenter smiled and pointed towards the boxes. 'Each one is a symbol of our success,' he said, his voice dropping to serious mode.

Unfortunately Derek did not pick up on the metaphoric implication of empty cardboard boxes and reacted negatively. 'What, empty boxes?'

His escort fumbled and strove to keep Derek on track. 'Ah...but they will eventually contain your livelihood, your ticket to freedom. So what's it to be – confectionary, fancy goods, adult requisites or cuddly toys?'

'Do I have to make a decision now?' Derek asked. 'I can't make my mind up between chocolates and cuddly toys.' Then his face lit up when he recalled wandering around amusement arcades as a child. 'I always fancied being the owner of one of them machines. You know, they have a crane with a grab on it and what you have to do is pick up whatever you want, carry it and drop it down a chute. And do you know what happens next?' Derek said, his laughter almost uncontrolled.

The man was staring at the ceiling because he knew what was coming but he joined in to keep Derek happy.

'The grab opens just before it gets to the chute!' they said in harmony.

'It happens every time!'

The man coughed in an attempt to regain his authority. 'If I can help with your decision, will your good lady be helping in this venture?'

Derek nodded.

'Then in my experience it's got to be cuddly toys and novelties. With the chocolate option, you would probably eat most of your stock. So, if you would like to back your car further into the loading bay, we will get you ready for the next stage.'

'I want to do them machines with a crane and a grab,' Derek insisted, somewhat childishly.

'Yes, yes, OK, no problem. They have toys and fancy goods in them as well,' replied the man, who had now lost his artificial smile and had adopted the 'just going through the motions' procedure.

They filled the boot, the rear and passenger seats with boxes of cuddly toys and machines, then it was back to the classroom for the sessions on machine installation and maintenance.

Later in the afternoon, Derek found himself in a lay-by poring through the mountain of invoices, product order forms and exploded diagrams of the machines. The words 'fun, success and awesome' kept going round in his head as he ate the sandwiches provided by his wife.

He arrived back home very much down in the dumps. 'There's too much to get my head round. I'm used to concentrating on one thing at a time. All these forms – you know what I'm like with forms. They do my head in.'

Evelyn sat and listened and nodded at the appropriate moments. 'Welcome to the real world, Derek, the world of multi-tasking. You've had it easy up at the factory. Well, now it's just different, that's all. There's nobody else to worry about. All you have to do is take your time and go from one machine to another, have a coffee when you want to. There will be other people doing exactly the same, so you can talk to them. You won't be on your own.'

She reached across the table and held his hand. 'You'll be fine,' she smiled, and he smiled back.

The open road to success

It took Derek a while to get his body to accept that he would no longer be doing split shifts, late nights or early mornings but eventually he got into the routine of rising at what is considered to be the normal waking hour. The schedule of driving to the locations was organised by his wife who, as part of the team, was beginning to enjoy the job. Derek did the driving, loading the machines, emptying the cash boxes and checking for damage. To his delight, he was amazed at how little else there was to do. On days when the tedium got to him and he wanted to cheer himself up, he would set the machine to complete a test run. He had to stifle his laughter as the grab dropped the trinket just prior to reaching the chute.

'It works a treat, but with minor adjustments maybe it could get closer before it loses the prize,' he chuckled as the crane went back to the starting position.

For laughs, though, the task of counting the massive heap of pound coins on the kitchen table gave them the most pleasure. He and Evelyn grinned like Cheshire cats as they filled the plastic bags provided by the bank. 'I never realised how dirty money could be,' he said, looking down at his hands.

'Have you never heard of filthy lucre? The smell of money?' his wife replied, holding her palms to her nose. 'Well, it smells like this.'

'One for you, one for me and one for the company,' they sang as they stacked the bags.

The tuition pays off

Geoff had impressed George with his ability to gain access to the machines and empty the money out in less than two minutes. 'That's very good. I always knew that you would be good at this. OK, this coming Sunday I will accompany you on your first outing but after that you are on your own, so get it right.'

'Sunday? Sunday is a day of rest!'

'The machines will be bursting with money. They've been sitting there all week plus the weekend, so we get to them before the man comes round on Monday.'

'Suppose so. But Sunday is lunchtime with my mates in the pub with football on the big screen. It's kind of a tradition.'

'Do you want to get rich or what?' George demanded. 'In any case, you can still go to the pub with your mates because we're going out after dark. You OK with that?'

'Yes, OK. No problem.' However, on the night Geoff was shaking like a leaf and had massive misgivings.

'You OK?' George asked, as he noticed concern written across Geoff's face.

'Yeah. It's just that I'm all right getting into the machines, it's the other bit I'm not sure about.'

'The other bit?' George queried.

'Yeah you know...the thieving bit.'

George pulled the car into a lay-by and switched off the engine. He turned sideways in his seat without letting go of the steering wheel. They sat for a moment with the street lamp lifting the light level up to gloomy.

Finally Gorge spoke. 'When we first discussed this arrangement, you do remember me saying that this is rich pickings and, as such, we should have no qualms in getting our share of the takings? There's loads to go around. It's not as though we're going to bankrupt anyone because, as I keep saying, we are selective. We choose only the machines that are within our grasp. There will be loads of others left. Follow my guidelines and you won't get caught or get questioned.'

Geoff sat upright; the pep talk appeared to have settled his nerves. 'Let's do it,' he said positively.

They pulled off the motorway and onto the half-empty services' car park. George got out his plan indicating the location of the machines. Circled on the plan were the machines to be emptied. 'Always read the plan and look at the circles. We do not rob the same machine twice within a two-month period. Now then, have a walk round, go to the gents, make out you are just a weary traveller, then come back and we will do it.' George rubbed his hands and smiled at Geoff.

Geoff walked through the mall, trying not to be conspicuous. He became aware that the power unit and cash bag were bulging in his inside pocket so he stopped, looked in the window of a closed shop and adjusted his clothing. He glanced around; nobody was watching. After a quick look at the plan, he located the alleyway, spotted the machine then nonchalantly walked back to the car.

George opened the passenger door for him as he neared the car. 'Don't get in. Go and do it. I'll be waiting here.'

Geoff could feel his heart thumping in his chest. He walked smartly back down the mall and turned into the alley where the machine was located then stood in front of it. Minutes later he was sitting in the passenger seat with a grin on his face, holding up a bulging bag of coins. 'Hey, that was easy. Where's the next one?'

'Look at the plan,' George replied, putting his foot down hard on the accelerator.

The smell of death and disinfectant

Digger and Spade had been invited to the mortuary to hear the opinion of the pathologist. 'Why do we have to go?' grumbled Spade. 'You know I can't stand the sight of blood.'

'You'll be OK, then. According to what I've heard, there's very little blood left. It's mostly slimy sloppy stuff. Look, we have to go because he wants us to see what his every-day tasks are. Plus, of course, he wants to see one of us throw up.'

The mortuary had similarities to an abattoir with its white tiles and stainless steel, but the smell was different. Spade was hardly through the door before he was holding his hand over his mouth and nose. 'God, what is it?' he muttered behind his palm.

'Strong disinfectant and death,' replied Digger with a slightly ghoulish accent.

The overweight pathologist smiled as they entered and beckoned them over to two stainless-steel tables, one containing a head and no body, the other containing a body and no head.

Spade waved his hands in submission and left before he brought up his breakfast.

'You'll clean up after yourself, won't you?' shouted the pathologist.

'Make it quick or I'll be joining him,' added Digger, looking up at the ceiling.

'So you've noticed that they are on separate tables.'

'So?'

'That's because they are not a match,' the pathologist informed him. 'Unrecognisable as they are, they do not belong to one another. Both male, both eaten away by something, and it's going to be a while before I can tell you any more.'

'You could have told us that on the phone.'

'I could have, but then the day would have been boring. Like as not, I wouldn't have spoken to anyone else all morning. So you see, just by your very presence you have made an old man very happy. Make sure your colleague cleans up, won't you?'

Outside, beyond the carpark, Digger spotted his colleague leaning against a tree. Spade waved a hanky then wiped the tears from his eyes. As they met, he wrinkled his nose. 'Oh God, you smell like the bloody mortuary,' he said. And with that, he went around the other side of the tree and heaved again.

Digger went to the car, put his overcoat in the boot and waited for Spade to recover. When he arrived, Digger related the pathologist's findings.

'You are joking!' Spade exclaimed. 'That means there's another head and another body...somewhere.'

'Yes, and unfortunately I think we have to revisit number two on your "Places I Hate Visiting" list.'

Digger had to agree with Spade that the smell from the mortuary had leeched into his overcoat and was taking over the car. It was convenient that it took a while for Spade to regain his composure because the delay in detectoring provided Digger with an opportunity to drop off his coat at the dry cleaners, to the dismay of the lady behind the counter.

'Sodding hell,' she gasped loudly as he took the coat out of the plastic bag. 'Where have you been – down a sewer? I'm not sure we can take this. Everything what goes near it will stink the same.'

Digger stared at her. 'Are you going to take it, or what?' he asked calmly.

'I'm not sure, I'll have to see the boss.' There was a pause then she turned and, without any care for the customers feelings, shouted loudly, 'Alice, there's a man here with a coat that stinks to high heaven. Are we alright to take it?'

Digger turned to the other customers who were waiting to be served, held out his arms and smiled as Alice came theatrically through a curtain behind the shop counter. She took hold of the collar and held up the coat. A customer who got a nose full of the odour left quickly.

'There's no stains on it, it just smells,' confirmed Alice. 'What have you been doing?' she probed further.

'Look, before you ruin my reputation any further, I am Inspector Digger. I have just been to the mortuary and now my coat has picked up some of the odours. Are you going to clean it or what?'

'We'll have to hang it outside for a couple of hours first.'

'Good. Give me a ticket...please.'

Outside the dry cleaners, Digger put the ticket in his wallet and noticed strangers stopping and staring at him. He surmised that word must have spread quickly about the smelly coat. 'Can I help you?' he barked.

Back in the car, Spade had recovered and he laughed when Digger told him about the dry cleaner incident. 'Do you know, I'm sure I can still smell the mortuary on you?' He opened the window on his side and gave exaggerated deep breaths and coughs.

'OK, OK,' Digger protested. 'It's not that bad – is it?'

Spade refused to wind up his window until they arrived at the mill. They spotted a space that read 'Visitors Only'.

'That's us then. Makes a nice change to be able to park on the factory grounds,' added Digger, as they walked to the reception area.

Almost as soon as they arrived, the sliding window opened smartly and noisily hit the jamb. The bespectacled lady-secretary's head filled the window. 'Oh hello. You again. We heard about your visit when we were shut. What do you want this time?'

The detectives were taken aback by her attitude; they smiled to one another then retaliated. 'Some civility will do for starters – unless you want to do this interview down at the station, where you might have to get a solicitor and wait three hours in a holding cell,' Spade retorted. 'It'll not do your reputation any good, people seeing you led away sobbing and in handcuffs... So civility or cuffs? What is it to be?' He grinned.

Another lady, who had been eavesdropping, interjected. 'Sorry about this, she's had a bad day. I'm Gillian. What can I do for you?'

'Five minutes of your time, that's all, and then we would like to have a walk around the building, if that's OK.'

They went into a dimly lit side office furnished with one table, four chairs and a phone. Spade looked up at the central light with its enamelled metal-dish shade and pulled the lapels of his jacket together as if he were chilly. 'Is this where they get the hard word? It's like a Cold War interrogation cell,' he said, attempting to lighten the atmosphere.

'No, it's for anything really, interviews or seeing reps,' Gillian said.

'Do you know why we are here?'

'Not really. It seems a bit heavy handed, the police coming round all the time about the trouble with the redundancies. I mean, there's been no complaints or crimes committed, not that I know of.'

'We're not here about the redundancies,' Digger said. 'We are here about a body being found in the canal. We are trying to identify who it is.'

'Who *they* are,' added Spade.

'Yes, that's right,' Digger agreed. 'There are two bodies – well, to be more precise, two sets of body parts from different bodies, that is. So we are here to find out if any of your staff have gone missing. Not redundant, not on holiday, just gone missing. We are trying to find out if there was any bad feeling that might have got out of hand. You know, threats of violence, particularly as we understand that some were made redundant and some were not.'

'People come and go all the time here, we can't keep track. It's the owner, Mr Granville, he really is peculiar. He doesn't tell us anything. We only get to know ages down the line, weeks after someone has left.' At that moment Gillian stood up, put her hand to her mouth and looked around the room. 'Sorry, I've said too much. I didn't mean it, honest. I can't help you any more.' Holding the sides of her face, she left hastily.

The police officers looked at one another, amazed at her speedy exit. Then, as if an old-fashioned penny had dropped from a great height, they smiled and ran their hands under the table and the chairs.

Spade shook his head. 'Well, there's nothing else here apart from the phone,' he mouthed without actually making a sound. He picked up the telephone, ensuring the receiver remained on its rest, then carefully turned it over. A small microphone was glued to the plastic base.

He replaced the apparatus on the table, pointed to the door and he and Digger left silently.

They walked through the reception and waved through the small sliding window. The lady they had spoken to, Gillian, waved them away with tears in her eyes.

'She'll lose her job. It's a shame,' Spade said. 'It's not supposed to happen. Can you believe a boss bugging the room? He must be a real control freak. Fancy not trusting your own staff.'

'Would you?' Digger asked sceptically.

'Ah, but is he a bad enough control freak to get shut of employees that get in his way?'

'Is that a question or a statement?'

'OK, a quick look in the factory – but only a quick look. I'm not sure I like the way this case is developing,' Spade said.

They walked in through the small doorway and then through floppy plastic doors into the production area. Spade pulled hard at Digger's jacket, directing him behind a pallet of goods ready to be shipped. 'Look, over there! Is he scary or what?'

'Jesus, he's like something out of a horror film.'

A man clad totally in rubber was ambling towards the container of caustic soda. He looked up at the sight glass, rubbed it with a rag to clarify the level of the contents then, obviously satisfied at what he had seen, nodded to himself and set off back down the walkway, splashing as he went.

'I can't believe it, that stuff is so dodgy.'

'Oh for fuck's sake,' Spade exclaimed looking down at the floor. Drips from the base of the tank had accumulated into puddles at the side of the walkway. 'Is that water or "you know what"?'

'Bugger. We need to get our shoes rinsed and quick,' Digger said with alarm in his voice.

'There's puddles of rain in the car park. Come on.'

They hastily went into the car park and each found a puddle. With the hope that this would remove, or at best dilute, the 'you-know-what' substance, they danced and splashed until their shoes and the bottoms of their trousers were soaked. When the dancing was over, a quick glance down confirmed that they had indeed soaked their trouser bottoms and shoes.

'I'm sopping wet. I told you this was going all wrong. Well, I hope it's done the trick because these shoes are ruined,' Digger said.

It was then that he heard applause and female tittering. He looked toward the main entrance; as it was the end of the working day, the departing office staff had stopped to observe the performance. One lady summed it up. 'You're either going back to your childhood or you've stood in something you shouldn't have.'

An investment strategy

Derek had had a good week. He had amassed a mountain of one-pound coins and just looking at them thrilled him. Evelyn had caught him running his fingers through the coins so he'd had to stop doing that. The problem was that he could not decide whether to pay them into the bank, use them for shopping, or bury them in the garden. He had tried paying for petrol and goods with them, but shopkeepers eyed him with suspicion. Another problem was the weight; he'd had to buy specially reinforced sacks because the coins were so heavy.

He suggested that, when things settled down after all the worry of the past few weeks, he and Evelyn should go on a holiday but the thought of carrying eight hundred pound coins into the travel agents was a bit embarrassing.

These issues were new to him and he had not yet found an answer. 'What do you do with all this money besides buy more stock?' He mulled it over as he looked at the pile of boxed cuddly toys in his garage. A smile broke out on his face as he moved the stock into a neater, more aligned arrangement on the shelf. 'An entrepreneur. Who would have thought it? Me – a new career, a self-employed businessman. I might have to get a suit – but will a tailor take pound coins?' he wondered as he switched off the light.

At the kitchen table, Evelyn was going over the accounts and the machine location sheet. 'At some point you're going to have to pay some money into the bank. The account has to be in the black so you can buy more stock. We are using up the boxes at a fair rate and, according to my calculations, you will run out within a fortnight. And if you place an order, it takes over a week to arrive.'

'Yes, but if you pay the coins into the bank then it becomes official. People start asking questions. Apparently the bank has a duty to report people paying in lots of cash because they think you are money laundering. And what happens when the tax people find out? They could take away the profit and all of the pleasure.'

'Everyone has to pay tax, even entrepreneurs and self-employed businessmen,' his wife mumbled, smiling.

'Ah, but entrepreneurs have accountants to fiddle the tax for them.'

'Well maybe so … but we can't afford an accountant,' she said, getting shirty with him.

The thought of declaring the profit depressed him, so he announced a financial strategy. 'OK, we'll compromise. We'll put enough into the bank to pay for the stock and the rest we bury in the garden.' Thinking he had solved the issue, he filled the kettle.

'Oh? And what happened to the holiday?' Evelyn hollered.

'Bugger.'

Another man coining it

Geoff was going through a similar dilemma: he also had a mountain of pound coins that he was unsure what to do with. For the moment, he had stored them in metal boxes on a shelf in the garage.

'How come you get paid in pound coins?' Ange asked, prior to going to the shops. 'It's a real pain. Everyone looks at you when you're counting them out.'

'Yes, I've had a word with George. Apparently he has a few machines out there himself, and he says it saves him going to the bank.'

His wife looked at him as if to suggest that it was a lame excuse and she knew she was being fobbed off. Truth was, he just took his cut in coins and brought them home in a large bag; he had not thought about the problem of how to pay for everyday goods. He had explained to Ange about the delight of stacking the boxes, each containing five hundred pounds, on the shelf and then simply looking at them. But she was not impressed by this either.

'Why do you work so late?' she enquired.

'That kind of night is it? A third-degree night?'

'No, it's just that when I explain to people what you do because they are interested, they don't understand why you work nights. And, come to think of it, neither do I.'

'How many more times? I work late because we are a service industry and, as such, we go into public places after the public has gone so that we don't upset the owners of the machines or the people who run the establishments. How many more times?!'

'No need to get grumpy, just seems a weird occupation, that's all.' After a pause, Ange set about him again. 'Is there just the two of you? If there were more, maybe you could come home earlier like normal people. You should put that to George, I'm sure he would understand.'

'Look, I've only been doing the job a matter of weeks. I can't go round telling him how to run his own business, can I?'

'Would you like me to have a word with him? This is a joint venture, after all.'

'No. I'm off to the garage.'

As the fluorescent light flickered on and illuminated his row of boxes, Geoff's mind drifted to other problems. 'God, it's only an old wooden garage and there's thousands on the shelf. What if some git finds out and breaks in? Fort Knox it isn't,' he said, rattling the flimsy door. He looked round at the rotting woodwork and corrugated asbestos roof. All of a sudden he panicked; he could not believe that he had stacked the money in there.

'What are you doing?' Ange asked, as he stood sweating in the kitchen having shifted all the boxes. They looked down at the tins of money. 'So what now? You can't leave them there.'

'I have to. It's only in the short term till I find somewhere more secure.'

'How much is there? Looks like a lot to say you've only been doing it a couple of weeks?'

'A couple of grand. I'll move it shortly, once I find a place,' he said in a low voice.

'A couple of grand?' she squealed. 'It is a lot. Mind you, once you have paid for an accountant, income tax and your expenses, it won't be that much, will it?'

'No, that's right,' Geoff barked, beginning to lose his temper.

'You will be doing it right, won't you? You know you have to declare it on your car insurance and all that other stuff. Only we don't want to get bitten on the arse. If you have an accident, your insurance will be void so they won't pay out. And then there's the police, if you don't declare it. You will, won't you?'

'Of course I will! What do you take me for?'

Just after dancing in the rain

The progress of the investigation into the two gruesome deaths was faltering; fortunately impetus came in the form of two size-ten shoes.

It had been a curious day, and the stress of all the events was beginning to take its toll on Sergeant Spade. He enjoyed his job, but groping around horrible factories and visiting morgues was not what he had signed up to do. He could be enthralled by a chase or catching a felon, but these were in short supply at the moment. So, as a means of switching off to the workaday crap, as he called it, he was relaxing in his favourite armchair watching the highlights of the snooker.

He had kicked his shoes off in the hallway in a feeble attempt not to get the carpet wet but unfortunately he'd ignored the moisture lurking in his socks. He sighed a relaxing sigh as he ripped the tag off a can of lager. He was allowing the froth to settle, whilst urging a black ball to drop in the middle pocket, when he felt his right foot tingle. He rubbed it with his other foot but it got worse.

Putting down the can, he bent forward and removed his sock to find blisters forming along the top of his toes and a feverish reddening on his foot. He checked his other foot to find the same thing happening. 'Soddin' hell.'

He had a suspicion about the cause of the condition and decided to immerse his foot in a bowl of cool water then phone a taxi to get him to hospital. Finally, he phoned Digger. 'I'm afraid the dancing in puddles didn't do the trick. That stuff must have soaked right through. Have you checked your feet? Only I'm off to the hospital.'

'I caught it earlier. I had a shower as soon as I got in, so my feet are OK. Just a tickle and a bit red, that's all, but my shoes have had it. I was going to phone to ask if you were affected.'

'Yeah, right, of course you were.'

'I was, it's just that I forgot. Look, I've had to bin my shoes and trousers but you have to be careful how you handle them. If it gets on your hands … well, you don't need me to tell you.'

'I better go get changed before I go. And I'll probably not be in tomorrow. But perhaps it's time we started asking some awkward questions. Got to go, the taxi's here.'

Spade opened the door and waved to the taxi. 'Won't be a minute,' he shouted. He was still wearing his work suit, so he dashed upstairs to put on some jeans then he wondered what to put on his feet. 'Can't put shoes on,' he muttered, looking down at the jumble of footwear in the hallway. He smiled as he picked up a pair of old slip-on house shoes. 'Should do the trick.'

He hobbled down the path, trying not to lose the slip-ons. The taxi driver looked him up and down. 'You OK? Only the sartorial elegance of your suit jacket and tie is ruined by the jeans and the choice of footwear.'

'Sore feet, that's all. The hospital please,' Spade replied, ignoring the pointed remark.

'Suppose it's an occupational hazard for coppers. You know, all that pounding the beat... You must go through some shoes.'

Spade sat back in the seat, unsure whether to continue with the conversation; luckily the chirpy taxi driver didn't give him chance to speak. As the man looked in his mirror and pulled away from the kerb, he offered an insight into his own ailments. 'We all get it you know, occupational wotsit. Mirror neck, from constantly turning your head. A rash...yeah a rash on your bum with sitting all day on these easy-clean seats. They make you sweat like crazy. Oh, and a fat belly from lack of exercise and too many bacon sarnies. So I do know how you feel.'

'Do you really?' muttered Spade.

He walked in to the reception area of the hospital outpatients and was immediately asked to fill in a form. As he worked his way through the personal details section, the receptionist asked a few simple questions. 'Occupation?'

'Policeman.'

She looked over the counter and admired his footwear. 'Nice slippers.' She smiled then beckoned a nurse; the laughter was infectious. 'We have a policeman here with sore feet.'

Soon the whole area was laughing, everyone except Spade who had moved to the waiting area and sat at the back next to the flat-screen TV that was showing the snooker.

'It's OK, I'll wait here till one of you condescends to take care of me. Just make sure you get here before my feet fall off,' he said, loud enough for them to hear.

***

After speaking to Spade, Digger had become a bit anxious about the case. Normally between them they could figure out what direction to take or who to speak to. Desperation was beginning to kick in; on top of that his boss, Chief Inspector Peacock, had been harassing him lately and Digger was getting concerned that it could affect his career. So, against his better instincts, he decided to take matters into his own hands. He went to his jacket, got out his notepad and flicked over the pages, scanning the scribbled comments.

'Not much to go on but there is only one place to visit. This time, however, I'll need a disguise and protection.'

He went to the garage and assessed the possibilities.' According to what I've seen, it has to be rubber, wellies, Marigolds, goggles and a waterproof jacket with a hood... safety first,' he muttered.

Digger parked his car amongst the other cars inside the factory perimeter. The illumination was low, with plenty of shadowy areas. 'Ideal for sneaking around,' he said to himself.

The nightshift was well underway when he arrived at the factory and, although he had been involved in undercover operations before, it was a long time ago. On this occasion he was on his own, which was against his better judgment and departmental rules.

As he approached the factory entrance, a conveniently recessed doorway allowed him to don his disguise. He put his everyday shoes and jacket in a holdall and stuffed it out of sight. If he had seen himself in a mirror, he might have opted for more sober colours but black wellies, blue waterproof walking pants, green jacket and yellow gloves were all he'd been able to find.

Wearing such bright colours meant it was difficult to hide, so he opted for the brazen approach. Walking with a purposeful gait, he made his way towards the production line. Uncannily, almost as soon as he had set off, the rubber-suited man plodded towards him. His rubber outfit was well used and, as he got closer, Digger struggled to see the eyes behind the scratched lenses of the helmet.

'Evening,' Digger said as they passed each other. Surprisingly, the man ignored him.

Pleasantries were not exchanged and Digger kept on walking. 'They all must dress like this,' he thought. He turned into a passageway and looked back. He watched as the man paused then glanced up to the sight glass of his favourite tank. Satisfied with what he saw, he opened a secluded doorway and walked through into a little workshop.

'Ah, he has a hidey hole,' Digger muttered. He shifted his position and hid behind a pallet of goods and waited. The rubber-suited man was a long time, so long that Digger started stamping his feet to offset the pins and needles that were setting in. 'He must be having a kip,' he thought.

Just when he was losing patience, the man came out. Digger watched him stretch as he exited as though he had just woken up; then, as the man passed the tank, he touched it affectionately.

'He really has a thing about that tank. Weird,' Digger thought.

He dropped out of sight as the man went by then looked at his watch. He hadn't a clue how long it would be before the man would return. 'Ten minutes max,' he muttered to himself.

He was eager to see what was inside the little room. As soon as the man had gone around the corner, Digger ran to the workshop, went inside and closed the door gently. It was a gloomy but cosy little workshop with a bench, a battered armchair, an electric fire and a tall wooden unit with drawers. Digger sniffed audibly: old oil, acid, warm rubber and strong body odour. 'Not often you get that combination,' he thought.

His hands were shaking as he rifled through the drawers. He wasn't sure what he was looking for. 'But it's what you do,' he hummed.

As he searched without success, his rummaging speeded up and his tidiness lessened. He opened a cupboard door and found row after row of jam jars, all labelled and filled with nuts, bolts, screws and other maintenance paraphernalia. On the top shelf he spotted a clean jar with no label. 'A new one,' he thought. He lifted it down and the hairs on the back of his neck bristled. Through the distorted glass, he could make out the eroded remains of two watches and two wedding rings, plus a couple of small glistening lumps. He shuddered, looked at his watch and stuffed the jar into his pocket.

Usually calm under pressure, it shocked him how nervous he was becoming. The shaky hands got worse and now beads of sweat on his forehead told him he should get out, and quickly. He glanced around. 'No time to tidy up,' he thought.

He opened the door – to be confronted by the rubber-suited man filling the door frame.

'Oh – what the fuck are you doing in here?' said the muffled voice from inside the helmet.

'Ah, glad I've caught you. We need more soda on the production line,' Digger blurted.

'I will decide if we need more soda. You should be on the packing line.'

There was a pause as the stand-off developed.

'What the fuck are you up to?' the man asked menacingly.

Digger was searching for words and he could hear his own voice trembling. 'They said go and get him to f-f-fetch more s-s-stuff, so here I am.'

The man in rubber looked him up and down. 'Are you new?'

'Yes. I don't know my way around proper yet, but I'm learning.'

'Well, you don't come in here. Now fuck off!'

'Certainly. Sorry to have bothered you. I'll go and tell them that you are on your way and that... Well, I'll be off then.'

Digger backed out of the workshop, keeping his hand over the top of the jar, and slowly walked towards the production line until he was sure the man had gone back into his hidey-hole. Then he turned and ran briskly for the door. He snatched his hold-all from the doorway as he went to the car park, flashed the car key and jumped in.

With the rear wheels spinning, he drove onto the main thoroughfare. He pushed the goggles and the hood back over his head and wiped away the sweat with his hanky. He blinked his eyes and pondered the last few minutes. 'Bloody hell, that was close. I'm not up to this confrontation business,' he said to the steering wheel.

He had only gone a mile or so when he noticed a blue light in his rear-view mirror. He also caught his reflection. 'Warrant card, wallet...in jacket at home. Shit,' he thought.

Pulling over in a lay-by, his mind raced. He sat trying to compose himself as the officer approached. Digger looked at the traffic officer through the driver's side window. 'God, he looks young and hard faced. This is not going to be easy,' he thought.

'You were a bit quick coming out of the side road just now. Step out of the car, sir,' said the officer.

Still wearing his disguise, Digger obeyed. 'Look, I know what you are thinking,' he said, realising he was still wearing the yellow rubber gloves.

'Then what am I thinking?'

'You are thinking what is a middle-aged man doing dressed like this, this late at night.'

'I'll tell you what I am thinking: I think you are on your way to a robbery. Or have committed one. Or you have been to a weird party. Have you consumed alcohol in the last hour, sir?' the young officer said as he took out his notepad.

Digger, exasperated, just blew into the air. 'Bleedin' hell.'

Further reflection on the late-night investigation

The following twenty-four hours were not easy for Digger, who had to explain his behaviour to everyone at the station. He had calmed down by the time Spade returned but still had to relate the entire story to him, which brought back the scariness of the occasion. 'I was so lucky. The rubber-suited bloke is enormous.'

Spade was laughing so much, he had to hold on to his stomach. 'Don't tell me any more – it's hurting now,' he said, taking off his glasses and wiping his eyes. 'You know it has gone all around the station and, on top of that, the boss is not too chuffed either. Something about letting down the professionalism of the service. I say it's all in the line of duty but, anyway, you do know you could have ended up in the mixer? 'Cos Mr Rubber Suit doesn't look the type of bloke to mess about, and if he had known just who you are...well, it doesn't bear thinking about.'

'I know, I know. It was scary...I'm still shaking. And then getting stopped... Do you know, that young officer wouldn't believe anything I said, and he still hasn't apologised for putting me in handcuffs.'

When they had calmed down, they looked at the contents of the jam jar.

'They look a bit knackered now. The watch is half eaten away. The only bits that have survived are the thin rings and the funny bits of gold,' said Spade, as he rolled the contents around in the jar.

'Fillings,' muttered Digger.

'What?'

'Fillings, they're fillings. You know, out of teeth.'

'Bloody hell, this is getting worse,' Spade exclaimed. 'And, if you don't mind me saying so, a bit gruesome.'

'Aye, and what's more, because they've been in some acid or something they're untraceable. No DNA, no nothing.'

Spade scratched his head. 'This case is not going to be easy. I still can't believe it's happening in that sleepy shit-hole.'

'Looks like we'll have to do it the old-fashioned way and ask some hard questions.'

'OK, who's first?'

'Who's missing?' Digger asked with a smirk in his voice.

'Top down, the manager-stroke-chemist. Let's go see his missus.'

'Before we set off, how are your feet? Do you think you'll manage pounding the beat?'

'Funny you should ask,' Spade replied, wriggling his bare feet towards Digger. 'The doctor said I should get some fresh air to my feet to aid the healing process.'

Digger looked over with definite distaste at the display. 'Not sure this is the place to be doing that.'

'I've got to do it somewhere.'

'I'd prefer it if it wasn't here.'

They discussed their boss, Chief Inspector Peacock, 'the man in the glass bubble', according to Spade. 'You can see him but you cannot touch.' They had come to the conclusion that his assessment of their progress was based purely on the content of the information board in their office. In order to keep him off their backs, they ensured that the board was always full of photos of dead bodies, suspects and locations. To make it look even more impressive, they also included felt-tip pen detail, illegible notes, circles, arrows and highlights in various colours. In times when information was thin, they had been known to fill gaps with holiday snaps and shopping lists to avoid lengthy accusations of slow progress. They made sure that their desks were piled high with files, irrespective of content.

Their boss was ex-military and, as such, ran his day by a timetable. Digger looked at his watch. 'Get ready, he'll be in any moment...now.'

As he said the word 'now', a shadowy figure appeared at the frosted-glass door. It opened smartly and their impeccably dressed superior officer marched in. Peacock glanced at the board, the desks and the occupants. 'I can see you are hard at it, keep up the good work. Mm... strange odour in here. I'll get the caretaker to check the drains. Carry on.' And then he was gone.

'How much longer is he going to fall for this?' Spade asked, pointing towards the board, and at the same time twiddling his toes under the desk.

'He's fallen for it today, and that's all we should worry about. Put your socks on, open the windows and let's depart this cheesy-smelling office before the caretaker arrives.'

As they made their way down the stairs from their office, Spade kept hold of the handrail and winced as he put his weight on each foot. 'Still tender then?' enquired Digger as he waited for him.

'More fresh air needed' said Spade. Digger drove and Spade navigated; this was a reversal of roles.

'I could probably manage an emergency slow down,' Spade said, as Digger jerkily edged out into the traffic. 'You'll soon get used to using the clutch,' he laughed.

After a tortuous journey, they parked on the opposite side and one block down from the manager/chemist's house. It was a tactic they had used before. Digger had suggested that, if they were to get the best outcome from the visit, they should be in tune with the surroundings so an exercise in crime-scene observation was initiated to get the feel of the place before they entered.

Spade was viewing it from a different angle, though. 'Not cheap these. Buy one on a manager's wage, could you? I don't think so. I bet they got it for a snip at four hundred grand. Could do with a lick of paint, though.'

He craned his neck from inside the car and peered up the short, inclined drive. Staring at the roof of the house, Spade offered an insight into his experiences with structural repairs. 'It'll be a nightmare to put right in a few years. All them gulleys and valleys – in fact, there's a couple of slates that look like they're sliding down right now,' he said with authority.

Digger looked at him. 'We are supposed to be observing the mood of the housing environment to see if there are any obvious issues or clues as to why the absent person has not been reported missing. We are not writing an article for a house-buying magazine.'

As they got out of the car, Digger said what he was thinking. 'If you don't mind my saying, I think you might have a loose slate.'

'That's OK, but people should know about these things before they buy a house.'

They both started to laugh then noticed the manager's wife standing, arms folded outside the front door.

'Oh dear,' Digger muttered under his breath.

'I wondered when you would turn up,' she said. 'I've been watching you for ages. I thought you were burglars casing the joint. I was just about to call the police.'

They ignored her shouts of indignation and continued to the front door.

'Good job we came then. Can we continue this inside?' Spade said calmly.

As they walked into the house, Digger's eyes scanned the room. 'You haven't reported him missing?'

'That's because I'm not interested in where he is.'

'It has been a while. Are you not worried that he might have come to some harm?'

'No,' she replied curtly.

'So all is not well in the household? I can't help but notice the absence of wedding or holiday photos,' Digger queried.

'Correct. He's gone and I've had a clear out. Anything relating to him has gone to the tip. God knows where he's gone – and do you know what? I'm not interested if he ever comes back.'

'Can we sit down? Take the weight off our feet?' Spade grinned at Digger who looked at the ceiling. 'It seems less formal, that's all. We've no axe to grind, we are just trying to trace him. Simple.'

'Feel free, make yourself at home,' the manager's wife replied but remained standing.

Spade sat back on the settee, stretched his legs then continued. 'We were hoping you could help us locate him. They are worried about your husband's disappearance at the factory.'

She huffed at his comment. 'I'll bet they are! He told me he has to go to the factory in the evenings to look after the late shift. I believed him at first, then one night he comes back smelling sweeter than when he went out. So the next time I followed him. Turns out he's shagging a woman who works in the office. From now on he does not exist, as far as I am concerned.'

'OK... You think he's run off with this woman, then?' Digger asked.

'Well, he hasn't come back and he's not been seen. No phone calls, no nothing.'

'I see. Do you have any photos of him?'

'A photo of him laughing would be very useful,' butted in Spade.

'Why?' she replied whilst rummaging in a drawer.

'To compare with dental records that's all. Nothing sinister.'

She turned and looked at Spade with a mystified expression. 'I would say it's pretty sinister looking at someone's dental records in order to identify them, if that's all that's left.'

Spade backtracked. 'No, what we mean is we can eliminate him from other enquiries by comparing the dental records with other dental records. Nothing sinister.'

'You better go. I've got visitors shortly,' she said, walking towards the hallway. She held the front door open for them then slammed it shut after they went through.

After a couple of paces they turned, grinned, then paused on the drive and studied the photo. Digger made a pertinent comment. 'No gold teeth showing, so it's not going to be much use in identifying who is who. But all of a sudden we have another witness in the frame. The lady in the office, the secretary who was having the bad day, was probably reduced to tears about the disappearance of the manager-stroke-chemist-stroke-boyfriend. Things are finally looking up, and I don't mean roof repairs,' he added, chuckling.

Spade had quick look at the chimney stack. 'Needs pointing but nothing sinister. Let's go,' he laughed.

They climbed into the car and set up the satnav for the next address. 'I think we can call it a partial success, a step in the right direction,' uttered Digger, as he waited for a satellite connection.

'We didn't hit a brick wall,' added Spade.

'That's the last of the structural references … agreed?'

'Agreed.'

Another jerky journey had Spade hanging on to the seat belt.

'It's not that bad,' disputed Digger.

'You're not sitting where I am.'

Their investigations took them to the home of the next missing person on the list, the absent shop steward. Fortunately it was on the same housing estate and not that far away. This time, to avoid being noticed, they parked a bit further down the street to plan their script.

'Will you look at these houses? Just how does anyone afford to buy one of these?' Spade asked.

'I know. Bit posh for a shop steward. He must have robbed a bank or won the lottery.'

'Or married into money?' Spade queried bitterly.

They relaxed a moment to let their avarice subside.

'Of course, we mustn't let the raging envy get in the way of our investigation process. We must remain professional,' Spade said.

'That's correct, professional – even if they, that is two people, live in a four-bedroom detached house with en-suite in every bedroom, a massive drive with a double garage and a lawn you could play cricket on. Correct. We will remain professional in every way.'

'OK. Rant over with?' Spade asked.

Digger nodded his head, took a deep breath then went back to being a detective. 'Still seems strange to me why nobody has reported either of them missing.'

'Unfortunately shop stewards fall into the category of people most likely to be disliked in a workplace. The other employees see them as lefties and extremists, and the management see them as troublemakers. The shop stewards think they are doing the right thing by sticking up for the workers and sticking it up the management.'

'Do you know, neither of their partners have been on the phone?'

'Could be another playing away from home situation,' Spade mused. 'It seems common these days.'

'Not thought of that. Maybe you've hit on something there,' Digger said thoughtfully.

As they discussed the politics and peculiarities of the situation, a smartly dressed young man left the house by way of the tradesman's entrance at the rear. He closed the garden gate behind him, looked left and right to make sure the coast was clear, and then climbed into a red sports car parked opposite.

'Hello, hello, what's all this here?' sniggered Spade

'Have you any thoughts as to this covert exit?' asked Digger.

'Well, where do we start? Far too shifty to be the eldest son.'

'They have no kids.'

'Then it's got to be the washing machine man,' Spade speculated. 'They must have a washing machine?'

'Too well dressed – and where is his tool box?'

'Say no more. Let's go and ask those awkward questions.'

They rang the bell and waited, then rang the bell again. 'Perhaps she's loading the washing machine; you know, putting it to the test,' Spade mused.

'Top or front loader?'

'Got to be front, tops are old hat. Aha, what have we here?'

A figure appeared through the opaque glass of the front door. They could just make out a lady wrapped in a towelling robe. 'What?' she growled through the letterbox.

'Can we have a word?'

Before Digger could produce his identity card, the woman bawled through the letterbox again. 'Can't you read? It says no hawkers or cold callers.'

'What about hot callers?' asked Spade.

She opened the door as far as the security chain would allow then put her face to the gap. 'If you don't piss off, I'll phone the police.'

'That's the second time today. We are going to have to wear a uniform,' Spade muttered.

Digger held out his card and smiled. 'We'll save you cost of the call, if you like?'

'What do you want?'

'Whatever it is, we are not going to conduct our business on this side of the door.'

'You'll have to wait till I make myself decent,' she barked and slammed the door.

'We could be here a while,' Spade suggested through a stifled laugh.

'I heard that! Well, now you *will* be a while,' she replied, loud enough to be heard down the street.

'Some voice. She could get a job on a fish market.'

It was a pleasant afternoon. After Digger and Spade had enjoyed further discussion regarding the styles of roof and the potential repair bills, the front door opened. They walked down the hallway into the kitchen area and stood around a breakfast table.

Digger opened proceedings. 'He's missing.'

'Who is?'

'Oh come on, lady! Your husband, the shop steward at the factory.'

'Oh him. He wasn't my husband, we never got married.'

'He's been missing a couple of weeks and you didn't think to report it?'

'It's not the first time he's gone missing, he makes a habit of it. But I do appreciate that this time it's been longer than usual.'

Digger looked at her closely. 'You seem to be taking it very well. In fact, you seem to have got over the loss very quickly.'

'Loss? Don't make me laugh! He was a waster, always on the cadge. I couldn't leave any money about or else he would pocket it.'

Spade looked around the kitchen; everything looked brand new. 'It's very smart in here, hardly used.'

'It's only for show,' the woman said. 'I don't go in for cooking. I eat out mostly.'

'Who was the chap who just left? He seemed a bit furtive as he closed the garden gate.'

'Oh, him? Really? No, he was just here to service the boiler.'

Digger turned and glanced at the gleaming, white, central-heating unit on the wall. 'He didn't have any tools with him.'

'No, he said he didn't need tools. He said it just needed resetting.'

'Really?' added Spade, turning to the kitchen window to hide his amusement.

'Do you have a photo of him?' asked Digger.

'Who, the boiler-repair man?'

'No, the shop-steward chap, the one who is missing, who isn't your husband.'

She stood back and put her hands on her hips before spelling it out. 'Now, look. For clarification, yes, I might have a picture of him on my phone. But as far as I am concerned, he's not missing from my life. He's just gone, gone into thin air – and I couldn't care less.'

Turning to a side table, she grabbed her phone. After a moment's swiping and pressing, she handed it to Digger, who expanded the image with two of his fingers. He smiled and passed it to Spade. 'Will you look at those teeth? Like a row of gravestones – and there's been a lot spent on dentistry.'

'Aye, and guess who paid for it?' the woman demanded.

'Can you forward the image to this number?' Digger added, as he handed over a calling card.

Outside, Spade elbowed Digger in the ribs and offered an aside. 'We could give her the jam jar so she could get her money back.'

'I bet she paid for the watch as well.'

A day of two halves

Derek was beginning to loosen up about his new job. It surprised him how quickly he had forgotten about working in the factory. He'd always thought he would work there until he retired, so it had come as an enormous shock when he was given the envelope containing his pay off. He still shuddered when people asked about the redundancy, even if it was done in a caring, sharing way, but he covered that by shouting, 'I've moved on since then.'

He bumped into a chap who he'd worked with on the night shift and told him it was the best move he had ever made. He was a bit reluctant to divulge exactly what he was doing, so skirted around the question.

His confidence was building each day and he was actually starting to enjoy setting off to work. 'Curious,' he remarked to himself. 'I never whistled when I was setting off to the factory.'

He climbed into his vehicle, which was laden with cuddly toys and machines, and read the job sheet provided by the company and put into plain English by his wife. 'Seems straightforward enough,' he said, setting the satnav and letting the other lady in his life guide him to his destination.

He had become quite fond of the navigation system's feminine tone and regarded her as a business partner on long journeys. He acknowledged her advice and thanked her openly when she suggested there was a speed restriction in the area; in areas where he was familiar with the route, they could get into a heated discussion regarding the most efficient direction to go. Her indignation was expressed by 'Recalculating... recalculating', in a voice that seemed get louder and angrier, and he would have to justify his manoeuvre in detail. The good news was that he was never late because the satnav woman always greeted him with 'Arriving at destination' in a cheerful manner.

On his rounds, he got to know the other coin-slot servicemen – or vending-machine managers, as they preferred to be addressed. Initially it was just a nod of the head to acknowledge a fellow service person; later the usual discussions would ensue regarding the many alternative, and usually foreign, coins that would dispense the commodity at a cheaper rate than was required.

On this occasion though, the other 'entrepreneur', Trevor, appeared despondent and angry.

'You OK?' Derek asked, as he watched the man sweep up the remains of the clear plastic window that allowed customers to view his array of goods. The window had obviously been smashed.

'No, I'm not. Do you know how much these things cost to put right? Not to mention the loss of the toys and cash.'

'Er no. Well, er, yes. Is there anything I can do to help?' Derek asked, stooping down to his level.

'No thanks, it's OK. I'm just a bit pissed off. This is the second time this has happened in as many weeks and you get no help from here.'

'Surely they can see them on CCTV. There's one over there.' Derek pointed to a camera.

'They couldn't give a shit here,' Trevor said bitterly. 'They won't even look at the recording. They say it's my machine so it's my problem.'

'Oh, I didn't know it was like that. I thought they would help you out. After all, they take a share of the profits.'

'Welcome to the world of cut-throat business and the lack of compassion.'

The wind fell out of Derek's sails as he listened to Trevor's travails whilst he put the remains of his machine into a plastic bag. 'It's about the location. No problem if your machine is in the middle of the walkway because there are lots of people about. But if it's like this one, tucked away in an alcove, you'll get done every week. So be wary about where you put them. I'm going to have to shift this one but all the best spaces have been taken. I fancy a coffee first. What do you reckon?'

'Yes, good idea,' Derek replied half-heartedly. He wanted to support Trevor in his hour of need but instead he was systematically going down his list of machines and assessing their location. His mindset went from elated optimism to desperate anxiety in a matter of minutes.

When Derek got home, Evelyn greeted him with a smile but was immediately aware that all was not well. They sat at the kitchen table, observing the layout of the locations of the machines. Derek pointed with a pen then circled the ones that he thought were vulnerable. 'I didn't realise there was a method to this. Apparently locations where people are always passing and that are near a camera are like gold dust. I thought it was a sales thing that these positions were crammed with other machines, but it's about security. I never thought that there were people out there that break into them.'

His wife held his hand across a pile of one-pound coins. 'Don't worry. Do as the man suggested and make sure that our machines are in a safe place.'

'When I set off this morning, I was happy as anything. Now I'm worrying about what's happening to the machines when I'm not there. Oh piss, this has gone badly wrong,' he said sadly.

But it wasn't just during the day that Derek had negative vibes. When he worked at the factory his sleep pattern was notorious: as soon as his head hit the pillow, he was off and he didn't wake until the alarm sounded. Self-employment had changed all of that. He would resist going to bed until late but even then he had difficulty getting to sleep and within hours he was staring at the ceiling. He enjoyed the practical side of his new job but the administrative details and financial worries affected him greatly. In the small hours, his thoughts flitted from the loss of the ten grand to worry about fluctuating income, and now it was the security issue and the location of the machines.

The discussion he'd had with the Trevor had altered everything. All Derek owned in the coin-slot business was out there: the machines, the product and the cash. They were all at the risk of vandalism and theft from opportunist yobs and, at the moment, he hadn't recouped his outlay.

Within days his behaviour changed: he was tired, short tempered and angry. And he could still hear his Evelyn's cautionary advice, 'Go and get a proper job,' and her threat that, 'If you blow it... I'll kill you.'

Single or double oven? That is the question

Geoff's wife, Ange, had decided to strike while the iron was hot or rather, in her words, 'spend the five grand whilst you've still got it'. She had wanted a new kitchen for years but every time she'd raised the topic with Geoff, it was the same reply: 'We can't afford it.'

'Well, now we can,' she said, smiling.

Several planners had walked around with tape measures giving their thoughts on the best method to convert a cubby hole into a spacious state-of-the-art kitchen. After studying endless examples of worktops, door fronts and handles, Ange decided to go for a complete change with marble tops, inset lights and built-in multi-oven units. She was ecstatic; Geoff was not. He still hadn't found a place to store the tins containing thousands of pound coins. He had moved the very heavy containers out of the rickety garage and hidden them in the old units in the kitchen; they were too heavy to move upstairs. So, where *does* one put tea caddies full of money?

'Where are we going to put them?' he asked, on finding out Ange's plans for the kitchen.

'I don't know, but if you're not going to put it in the bank like normal people...'

'OK, in the short term I'll split the tins down to smaller amounts, put some back in the garage and some upstairs in the bedroom. The rest I'll put in the bank and, if they ask, I'll say we have emptied a piggy bank.'

'OK, but only in the short term. I'm not having old tins cluttering up the bedroom. I want us to be proud of this house. I want to invite people in and not be embarrassed by the crap furniture. I was thinking about having a kitchen-warming party when it's finished. What do you think? You could invite your friends and George.'

'Really? I had thought about spending the five grand on a new garage, but you beat me to it.'

As she moved towards him, Ange grabbed a large frying pan by the handle.

'Only joking,' Geoff said, holding his hands out in defence.

'I'll bet you are,' she replied with an irritation in her voice that he had not heard before.

Later that day, he was outside with a tape measure. He made a note of the dimensions then dialled his mobile. 'Yes, a quote for a prefabricated garage, erected on site. That's OK – and it's up to me to sort out the concrete base? No problem, I'll get back to you.' He smiled and put his phone away. 'All I have to do now is wait for an opportune moment.'

An unwelcome visitor

Digger had not quite got over the incident of the night shift. It had been a few days since the frightening occasion and he thought that by now he should have forgotten it all, but going round in his mind was the 'what if?'. What if the man in the rubber suit had come back sooner? What if the man had not believed his story about working there? What if the car had refused to start? What if the rubber-suited man had caught him?

He was sitting in the lounge, sweating and trying to watch meaningless television in an effort to take his mind of it. It was then that he realised he had developed a twitch in his right eyelid. 'Well, I am tired,' he reasoned.

He held his eye with his finger to try and stabilise the movement but his finger was trembling too. His state of mind had also been affected after a severe reprimand from his superior about procedures regarding risky investigations on suspects' property. He felt as though his credibility had waned somewhat. After all, in his mind he was the main man; he did not get chastised.

It was times like these that Digger assumed he could always rely on his wife, Irene for sound advice and support. He thought she would see it his way but, unfortunately, she poured salt into the open wound. 'You went out wearing that? Are you mad?' she remarked incredulously.

Irene expressed amazement when she found the pile of soiled, multi-coloured apparel on the kitchen floor. He'd tried to explain but he was tired and upset and, if he had told her the truth about pursuing an acid-bath murderer into the place where the slaughter had probably happened, he knew another bollocking would be on its way. So he fobbed her off with the usual statement: 'I cannot discuss the details of an ongoing investigation.' But she saw straight through it.

'You're in your fifties, you'll be retiring soon, and here you go playing silly buggers. If you get hurt, well... We need to enjoy our retirement and I'm not pushing you around in a wheelchair.'

He turned towards her. He had hoped for some kind of help, maybe a cuddle or a comment that suggested he was doing a fantastic job under extreme circumstances, but none was forthcoming. There was an expectant pause, an impasse. 'Thanks,' he said morosely. 'If that's the best you can do, I'm off to bed.'

Digger left her watching the late-night news and trudged out of the room. He went through his usual bathroom routine and then found himself staring into the mirror, watching his twitching eyelid. 'Fuck's wrong with it?' he grunted.

He tossed and turned for quite some time before he eventually dozed off. Irene, who had eventually followed him upstairs, decided on a book she was half-way through and left the bedside light on. She watched as he nervously jerked and breathed heavily.

About an hour later, he sat bolt upright and his eyes flashed open. He turned an ear towards the window. 'Did you hear that?' he shouted. Despite the volume of his enquiry, his wife slept on, unaware of his alarm.

The bedside light was off. So as not to disturb her, Digger carefully peeled back the bedclothes and slid from under the sheets. Edging his way in the darkness, he made his way downstairs and into the kitchen. He went towards the back door, muttering about animals and nocturnal goings-on. Confident that the cause of the disturbance was next door's cat, he stepped out through the door. A smell he recognised wafted up his nostrils. 'Warm rubber, acid, old oil and body odour. Fuck.'

Before he could step back into the security of the kitchen, a hot and slippery rubber hand gripped him around his throat and pinned him against the wall. Digger could not speak; he just saw glaring, bloodshot eyes within the rubber helmet.

And then a gruff voice put him in the picture. 'Did you think I wouldn't find you, you bastard? Now where is my jam jar?'

The grip around Digger's throat tightened then slackened to allow him to speak. 'I haven't got it! I haven't got your bleeding jam jar,' he croaked.

The rubber-suited man shook him like a rag doll. 'Where is it, where is it?' His voice boomed as he got angrier.

'I haven't got it...I haven't got it,' Digger screamed louder. He felt as though he was being rattled to bits, then more shaking, then…

'Stop it you bloody fool, you'll waken the whole street,' Irene yelled, shaking him by the shoulders.

He sat upright, coughing and bathed in sweat, and looked around the room as if the man were hiding somewhere. Still in a panic, he threw back the damp bedsheets then turned and sat on the edge of the bed, holding his throbbing head with one hand and his throat with the other.

His wife sat beside him smirking. 'So what is in the jam jar? And what have you done with it?' she queried with a cackle in her voice.

'Strong tea, a chocolate digestive and a shower,' he said hoarsely.

Digger met Spade the following day and told him about the nightmare. He was still trembling as he described being grabbed by the throat; he added choking noises to emphasise the story. 'Do you know, I can still smell it? I can't get the stench from out of my nose.'

Spade listened but, as usual, he saw the funny side and offered little sympathy. 'Are you sure it wasn't your wife? Ages ago, I seem to remember her saying to you that if you carried on like that, she'd strangle you. It could have been because she has a wicked sense of humour.'

Digger smiled for the first time in twenty-four hours. 'Yeh, yeh, thanks for the support. You and my wife should get together.'

'It's right. You probably just had too much cheese and red wine. Anyway there's only one way to sort this – we have to catch the bastard... But first we have to sort your nose.'

Digger looked at him curiously.

Splendid surroundings

They made their way to the cafe and, upon entering, lifted their noses high to savour the aroma of freshly-ground coffee beans. Since the lecture from their superior, Chief Inspector Peacock, they had decided to take his words literally and spend the time, as he put it, 'detectering in the field', i.e. the cafe.

They proceeded to their favourite spot, nodding to the waitresses as they went past the counter. The mock-Italian surroundings appealed to them: dark-oak panelling with wall hangings showing scooters ridden by people in suits and dark glasses; leather armchairs, and a round coffee table just big enough to take all the coffee paraphernalia and detectoring accoutrements.

It had taken a few visits before they decided on the ideal location. 'We need to see but not be seen,' was Digger's way of putting it.

They waited until the cups of Columbian arrived then Digger opened the meeting. 'We know who the dead are because we have what's left of them. What we don't know is the MO.'

Spade reclined to the back of his chair and dreamed. 'MO, ah yes, *modus operandi*. It takes me back to the police academy, *modus operandi*. The procedure, why and how would somebody would want to do it.'

'Precisely. And if we don't get our skates on, this case will go as cold as this coffee.'

'I told you, you should have ordered hot milk. Besides, I quite like it here watching the goings on,' said Spade, relaxing further.

Suddenly Digger leaned forward and put his hand on the arm of Spade's chair. He was just about to say something vitally important and confidential when he noticed the waitress standing by the table. There was a pause as he looked up at her.

'Go on, finish you're whispering,' she said. 'I just wanted to know if you would like a refill.'

Digger observed the empty cups and sighed. 'Yes, that would be fine. And I am not whispering, not in the sense that you mean. You were implying that I was saying something affectionate to my colleague here, when in fact he is a work colleague. We get on, but only in the way work colleagues get on, if you get my drift.'

'Bloody hell, touchy or what? Do you want a refill?' the waitress repeated but a bit louder. She reluctantly topped up their cups, then muttered expletives as she walked back to the counter. They let her get out of earshot and continued.

'Go on, then,' Spade laughed.

'Don't turn round but the woman over there, the one with her back to us, is the one we interviewed at the factory. Shouldn't she be at work?'

'It happened then. The bug, it must have worked. When her boss heard her talking to us, she got the sack. Maybe she will be a bit more open about her experiences at work.'

'Personally, if it were me, I'd be a bit pissed off having lost my job and less inclined to help the police – but then that's only me,' Digger said. 'Only one way to find out, Spade. We need to talk to her. You have a magnetic personality – go and invite her over to our interview table.'

'Me?' Spade slid out of his chair and half-heartedly made his way to where the woman was sitting. She was reading the texts on her phone and failed to notice his presence, so he moved closer, stooping low to catch her attention. When she eventually spotted him, she gasped audibly. He had his words planned but the order of saying them deserted him. 'Sorry you got the sack.'

She turned and sneered. 'Oh God, what do you want?'

'Sorry, I didn't mean it like that. What I meant to say was that if you have lost your job, it is a travesty. Maybe we can help.'

'How?'

'Come over to our table and let me get you a coffee.' Spade guided her to the table, pulled out a chair then eased it in as she sat down.

'Sorry you got the sack,' said Digger.

'You bastards,' she hissed, then tried to stand but found she was hemmed in by the chair.

'No, no, he didn't mean it like that, did you, sir?' Spade protested.

'Er no, what I meant to say is, you are probably better off out of there,' Digger said. 'It must have been an awful place to work.'

'I still work there, you pair of shits. What's all this about?' she said bluntly.

'Oh, that's good. We thought that, with the bug and all…' stuttered Spade.

Digger exhaled and sat back. He wasn't sure which tack to take. 'Are you a latte person or do you like it stronger?'

'Actually I prefer tea, but coffee is OK.'

Spade returned after ordering the drinks and sat, not knowing what had been said. Digger leaned forward and put him in the picture. 'She, er, sorry – I've forgotten your name.'

'It's Gillian,' she said softly.

'Well, it's good news. Gillian here still works at the factory,' Digger added, turning to face Spade.

They all smiled then there was a break in conversation as the waitress arrived with the coffees; she also smiled, but in a curious way. As soon as everyone's cups had been filled, Gillian sought clarification. 'How come you are so happy that I'm still working at the factory?'

'We thought, wrongly as it turned out, that as our little chat in that room at the factory was bugged and whoever listened to the recording probably would not be too happy that you slagged them off. As a consequence, you might not work there any more.'

'I was lucky. We, that is the office staff, know about the bugs. The place is full of them. When I spoke to you, that one must have been switched off. But other bugs appear overnight. His favourite place is in the light fittings. When anyone spots a bug that we don't know about, we tell each other so that if we're having an iffy conversation we know where we should be standing.'

'His? Who is this "his" person?'

'The owner, Mr Granville. We think it's him, but nobody has ever seen him. He never comes in, he does all his dealings by text or email. We don't even know what he looks like.'

Spade sat back in his chair. 'But he must come in, mustn't he, if he fits the bugs? In fact, by the sound of it, I bet he comes in quite a lot.'

'Lillian – can I call you by your first name, Lillian? We have a proposition for you,' said Digger.

Spade spotted the error and inhaled loudly through his teeth to warn Digger.

'It's Gillian, my name is Gillian.'

'Sorry, sorry. Anyway, what do you think?'

'About what?'
'Well, it's like this...'

Now everyone looks shifty

The possibility of someone forcing an entry into his lovely machines had affected Derek in a curious way. Distrust had taken over and, as a result, he had acquired a new habit: he had become a body-language observer.

A trip to the local library had opened up a new area of interest for him; he'd had no idea that a nod or a wink could have other implications. The phrase 'non-verbal communication' had entered his thinking processes.

All of a sudden, members of the general public were guilty of machine tampering until proven innocent. When he had first taken on the business, he'd estimated that his rounds could be completed quickly, half a day maximum, with the rest of the time for himself. He could go fishing or bird watching, things he'd never had time for before. However, since becoming an observer of non-verbal communication, his time on customers' premises had more than doubled – especially if he was doubtful about a punter's honesty. Hiding in corners observing individuals who used the machines, and being ready to pounce if their behaviour overstepped the mark, could take all day.

Initially he was alerted to anyone who was wearing a hood or carrying an oversize bag but now he watched their faces for signs of stealth as they inserted their coins. Individuals who looked sideways as they stood in front of the machine were high on his list of potential opportunist thieves. Since reading the top twenty-five examples of body language indicators, he found that he had to observe their walking gait for confidence, and their hands being rubbed together indicating anticipation. Anyone standing with their hands on their hips was a potential thief because it indicated readiness and aggression. Of course, in order to observe these individuals meant he himself could be thought to be loitering...

The act of concealing himself in a corner or behind a pillar opposite one of his machines meant that he had unwittingly become number-one suspect in the eyes of the security-camera operator who had been told to look out for 'thieves operating in this area'. And, as his job entailed the observation of the general public for signs of foul play, he was also educated in the theory of body language and suspicious behaviour. He watched Derek for a while and decided that he ticked most boxes in the 'Observation of Suspicious Characters' manual; it was about time that they found out what he was up to.

Alerted by the security-camera observer, the security personnel closed in on the suspect. The highest-ranking member of the team signalled 'go, go, go', and his trusty troops rushed towards Derek and pinned him to the floor.

Customers hastily backed away from the scuffle. 'It's OK, no cause for alarm. We have just apprehended a suspect who was about to commit a crime,' the team leader reassured the cowering shoppers. 'Come quietly, sir. It is best for you. We don't want a scene, do we? Well done men, an efficient put down of the felon.'

The officer leaned forward and spoke threateningly in Derek's face. 'We've been watching you for ages. Just waiting for your opportunity, were you? Well, you're nicked.'

Derek allowed the ex-army sergeant to manhandle him to the manager's office. He decided they were not going to listen to his explanation, so he let them get on with it.

'In there,' said the bright-blue uniformed officer as Derek was bundled through the door. 'We got him, we caught him red handed. He was just about to rifle the machine.'

The manageress stood up from her seat and eyed them all. 'Derek, what on earth are you doing?'

'I was just looking after my machines, making sure that they don't get trashed like the one other day, when this lot turned up.'

The men released their grip on Derek and he regained his composure. Whilst straightening his clothing, he snarled, 'They could have done me a serious injury. If they could spot me, how come they missed the robbery the other day? Ask them that,' he grumbled, looking at the manageress then the security men.

'It's OK, you can go back to your stations,' the woman announced in a compassionate voice. 'This is Derek, he owns some of the machines down there.'

'Why didn't you say so and save us all this palaver?' replied the security officer as he dusted Derek's jacket down before hustling his men back to their posts.

Derek and the manageress remained silent until they had left, then she pointed to the seat. 'You can't keep going on like this, it'll make you ill.'

'I know but we have to catch them. We exist on a financial knife edge. A couple of break-ins and you're finished. Machines, stock and cash – it takes some recouping.'

'OK, from now on we will be more vigilant, I promise. Coffee?' she asked, turning to her personal, executive, coffee-making machine. 'Cappuccino?'

Derek eased back into the chrome-and-leather chair and a smile wafted across his face.

'A penny for them,' she said as she put down the cups.

'Six weeks ago I was filling soap moulds in a dirty, stinking mill. Who'd have thought it?'

She leaned forward, elbows on the desk, and smiled back. 'You've done very well. Your wife must be very proud of you.'

'I don't think proud is the word she would use.'

'Well, if you ever feel like chilling, you know... If it's getting too much, just pop up here and I'll make you a coffee. Consider it to be your refuge.'

'Bloody hell, I will.'

He arrived home and put the van at the top of the short drive. After climbing out, he attached the security padlock to the back door of the vehicle and displayed the poster that advised 'No tools are left in here overnight', even though they were.

His wife was at the sink with her back to him and didn't turn round. 'You're late. Tea is ruined – I've chucked it in the bin. Afraid its beans on toast. Can you make your own?'

'Crikey, OK,' he said softly as he pondered the day.

He sat for a moment and then realised he had not escaped unhurt as he was roughed up by the security guards. His arms ached where they had tried to put them behind him, and his knees and elbows were scuffed where they'd wrestled him to the floor.

He turned to see Evelyn standing in the doorway. 'You OK?' she asked.

'Fine, just fine. I'm going for a shower,' he replied with a hint of irritation in his voice.

'Suit yourself, I only asked.'

'I probably will,' he muttered as he trudged upstairs.

Hot desking

Almost at the same time that Derek set off upstairs to bed, Geoff's day was just beginning. Fully equipped and full of confidence, he climbed into his car. He was becoming familiar with the routes and felt as though he was dropping into a routine, so a quick scan of George's instructions and he was off.

In his spare time, he'd been visiting the gym in an attempt become swifter and lighter on his feet and to strengthen his arms and wrists. He hadn't realised initially, but the few weeks in his new occupation had taken their toll. He ached from drilling into the machines and carrying the coins, and worried that he was not fleeing the scene quickly enough. Explaining to the fitness-programme organiser at the gym why he wanted these improvements seemed awkward, so he settled for saying he wanted to be stronger and fitter, particularly his arms and legs.

A course of step-ups and weight training had been recommended, with warm-up and cool-down on the stationary bike. As he watched the clock whilst cycling, Geoff had time to reflect. He still wasn't fully convinced that being a robber for a living was his thing, and he still had sleepless nights worrying that he might get caught.

To try to settle his mind, he had come up with a short-term plan, a longer-term plan and then an exit. His short-term plan was to be the best, the most efficient and the least conspicuous thief in the business; the longer-term plan was to amass a certain amount of cash, maybe a hundred grand, and the exit was to simply walk way. 'Six months max, in simple maths,' he thought.

He counted the cash most nights and was pleased with the general trend, but its growth was slower than he'd anticipated. 'Only twenty grand? Thought it would be more than that by now,' he said to himself as he counted it again. 'Ange would ask first, wouldn't she? She wouldn't just help herself,' he thought, as he locked the garage door one night.

He was early at the first location and decided to park up and listen to the radio or read the paper until the vehicles dissipated and there were fewer people around. Finally, he looked at his watch then braced himself; he was familiar with the place and knew exactly where the machine was, so he marched in. 'Brisk but casual,' he reminded himself as he neared the machine.

He stood in front of it and sweat broke out over his entire body. It took what seemed like minutes, but was only seconds, for him to comprehend what he saw.

'Don't put any money in that. Some bastard's broken into it,' said a man wearing a brown smock and carrying a brush and shovel.

Geoff stood in a daze, hearing the man but not comprehending his words. He looked at the wreckage: shards of plastic on the floor, the machine bent and twisted, and the odd pound coin on the floor where it had rolled away. 'Not very professional,' he said to the cleaner.

The man did not follow Geoff's comment and carried on sweeping up. 'Whoever it was trashed the whole machine for a couple of quid. They must be desperate and they must have made a racket while they were at it. Of course, nobody sees or hears anything. Too busy with their own goings on,' he said.

'Let me help you.'

'No, better not, too many sharp edges. Thanks, anyway.'

Geoff walked away, confused. He felt sorry for the owner of the machine but, if it had not been robbed when he arrived, he would have robbed it himself. He looked at his list; the situation took on the feeling of a race. 'Better get to the next one … before the thief does.'

He tried not to run from the building but found it difficult. Twenty fraught minutes later he parked up, settled himself again and briskly walked in. He couldn't believe it! He could see them from a distance, the scraps on the floor next to the trashed machine. People walked past as though this was how it was supposed to be; they allowed their children to reach inside the shattered remains and run off with a trophy.

Sitting outside in his car, he shook his head in disbelief. 'Can't understand the situation I'm in. I'm chasing a robber who's ahead of me because I want to rob the machine before he does! Is this real?'

He phoned George, who also was shocked. 'You better come in and we'll talk about it. Don't worry, I'll sort it.'

Gone midnight, feeling tired and losing faith in the venture, Geoff entered the workshop. To his surprise George wasn't at all downbeat. 'There's a coffee ready for you over there,' he said, pointing to the brew area. 'When you're ready, bring it in here and we'll sort how we are going to fix this bastard.'

Geoff looked up and a 'ping' happened in his mind. 'Is this what the discussion is like after I've robbed a machine?' he wondered. Remorse set in.

Before he had chance to think too much, George put his arm round his shoulders and walked him into the office. 'Bit of a shock, but don't let it get to you. There are hundreds and hundreds of these machines all waiting for you. But first we settle a small score. Have you got your list?'

George compared the list to his master chart, then to a map of the area they worked in. He placed a felt-tipped marker dot on the robbed machines and let his finger follow the road. 'He's going north. If he's consistent, tomorrow he will be here,' he said, putting an X to mark the spot.

'What do we do?'

'You will be doing nothing, you are having a night off. But don't worry, it will all be sorted when you come back.'

Geoff set off home empty handed, unsure what he would tell Ange. 'I could say I was beaten to the machine by a robber,' he thought, but inside he hoped she would be fast asleep and he could slide in alongside her and that would be that. Apart from a grunt and a pull of the sheets it was, but he couldn't sleep; he was still shaking.

He tried to work out how George would sort out the situation. Geoff had only known him for a short while but already he was aware of a serious, probably vicious side to him.

'George is not going to ask him nicely not to break into the machines and he's not going to say, "Can I work with you or will you work with me?" And he won't pay him off. Not much left, other than violence or the threat of violence...and after that I've got to work alongside a man who thinks violence is just a way of life. Oh fuck!'

The poacher becomes the gamekeeper to Poacher Number Two

George set off on his mission to apprehend the individual who was scuppering the smooth operation of Coin-slot Repair, Maintenance and Robbery Ltd. It made him smile when he said that phrase to himself.

He was unsure exactly what time the person would arrive, so he got there early. He found a parking position that was inconspicuous but provided an unrestricted view of the entrances to the building where the machine was located that he believed would be targeted next. The weather was ideal that evening; it was overcast with moisture in the atmosphere, and there were dark shadows created by the tall lights.

In the expectation of a long night, he had brought a flask, sandwiches and his favourite crossword. He settled down with a classical music radio channel playing in the background and waited. The time passed slowly and, after a while, he began to think that he had got it wrong.

'Surely not,' he thought. So, to settle his mounting doubts, he went over his conclusions again. 'Whether this person is an opportunist or has a plan, he was moving north and this is the next location stacked with machines. There are others, but not with this many machines. It has to be here... Just got to be patient, that's all.' Happy with his reasoning, he settled back.

George ate his sandwiches, finished the crossword, and the radio was beginning to get on his nerves; more importantly, he was getting cold. He sat up, started the car and let the engine run for a while before turning on the heater. Suddenly he reached for the ignition and switched off the engine; exhaust fumes in the cold air had enveloped the car and he was sure it had raised awareness that he was there. He sat lower in his seat and hoped the cloud of white fumes would dissipate quickly.

As he waited, he spotted a hooded person hobbling towards a car. He looked closer; a large bulge under his jacket gave away the fact that the figure was struggling to carry a considerable weight. 'A pile of coins, maybe. They can be rather heavy and make you walk with a limp,' George thought. 'About time,' he muttered as he opened his door.

Lights flashed on a car, indicating where the person was heading. George pulled down his balaclava and headed towards it too. Keeping low behind the boot of the thief's car, he waited for him to arrive. As the man placed his hand on the door handle, George grabbed his other wrist, forced it up his back and held his head firmly on the car roof.

The thief felt cold moisture on the side of his face and, as he struggled, he glanced sideways and saw the large steel knife in George's hand glinting in the car-park lights. 'No,' he shouted as George stabbed him.

George pushed the knife in, then worked it upwards in jerking movements. The man threw back his head, expecting the worst. He had never been stabbed before and didn't really know what it would feel like. There was a pause. In slow motion, the man expected pain, blood and eventual death. He waited for these sensations to kick in; he imagined his legs buckling and his lifeless body sinking to the floor in a pool of his own blood. He waited for what seemed ages but in fact was only a split second then, strangely, a cold feeling ran down the side of his trousers, as if his body fluid was draining out of him.

'Oh, I'm done,' he gasped. He had read about bodily liquids being expelled during a shocking experience and thought that this was it: the end. He imagined the sleepy death throes, the gradual, helpless crumpling to the ground as his organs failed. He even imagined himself being found by the police in a heap under a hedge somewhere, and eventually being zipped inside a body bag and carted off to the morgue.

He opened his eyes. Moments passed as he tried to make sense of it all. He was still there, being held firmly against the car. Glancing down, he fully expected to be standing in a pool of his own blood but he was standing in a pile of coins. George had stabbed him in his money bag and the coins were dropping out, one by one, down the side of his legs. A flicker of a smile crossed the robber's face as he realised he was still alive and existing in this world.

George got close and gave out some advice. 'You're getting us a bad name. Broken plastic all over the place, coins on the floor – have you no respect for our profession and other people's property?' he hissed into the man's ear. 'You've been lucky but next time it will be you that feels the chill of the blade. Now fuck off back to where you came from and don't operate in at least a fifty-mile radius of here. Get it?'

The young man could not believe his good fortune; he grimaced manically and nodded acceptance of the terms, then slumped as George released his grip. A tear ran down his face as he comprehended just how close he had come to a nasty end. 'I didn't know... If you'd have said...' He started to speak but George was not for listening.

'Now go.'

The man gathered his thoughts then looked down longingly at the pile of shiny coins. Holding a palm towards them, he begged, 'It'd be a shame to leave them.'

'Not a chance. Just go,' George barked.

As the man drove away George, who was still wearing his balaclava, also looked at the money. He was in two minds but the twitchy movement of one of the cameras on a pole above suggested he should be on his way.

As he drove away, a car pulled in behind and parked over the pile of coins.

'That driver's sitting on a fortune,' George muttered.

It was just a matter of time

It was a normal day for Derek. The contents of the bags in the car had been swapped from toys to coins; he had one last venue to visit… 'Soon be home,' he thought.

He parked adjacent to the entrance then walked down the mall carrying his keys and equipment. A cleaner who he usually chatted with was looking the other way as he approached and kept on cleaning. Immediately Derek sensed all was not well. From a distance he saw that the shiny machine casing had dark hole in it. As he speeded towards the machine, his heart sank then raced, and then his head ached.

'Utter bastards,' he said, loud enough for passers-by to turn.

He looked through the hole. 'Empty! The bastards, not a fucking coin left!' he ranted. 'But *you knew*, didn't you? Didn't you?' he shouted towards the cleaner, who had ducked out of sight.

He checked over the machine. All was well with the crane and the toys were still there; it was only the casing that was damaged. He leant against the wall and stared, not knowing what to do. People sauntered past ignoring his plight, thinking he was a man just having a funny turn.

'So this is it – war. Them against me. Nothing is sacred from now on. They have run off with my livelihood,' Derek said to a half-interested shopper who walked quickly on.

It took him ten minutes or so to regain his composure and even then he was still shaking. He rummaged in his bag for the tools he needed to attend to the wreckage of his machine, but he had not expected to have to complete running repairs and hadn't the equipment. 'Best take it home,' he muttered through a haze of tears.

He dismantled the machine and, as he moved it, he spotted two pound coins. The rage inside him exploded. 'You forgot these, you bastards,' he shouted, as tears engulfed his face.

He had calmed down by the time he approached home but, as soon as he entered the house, Evelyn noticed his still-reddened face. 'What's happened?' she said, cuddling him on the threshold of the house.

'They have robbed one of the machines.'

'Who has?'

'I don't know. All I know is I turned up to empty the machine and all the money was gone. I can fix the machine. Problem is, the more I look at them, the more vulnerable they seem. It's obviously dead easy to get into them. I thought that it would be secure because it has a lock and I have the key, but I bet a screwdriver would do just as well.'

'Let me get you a cup of tea. I'm sure there is an answer – there always is.'

They drank their tea, not knowing what to say. Derek's mind flicked from revenge on the person who was stealing from the machine to methods of security: extra-large padlocks; alarms; notices on the machine indicating the level of security; electric shocks or special paint ejected on to the perpetrator.

His wife was unable to stand the silence. 'Maybe you can get help from factory. They supply the machines and I bet they've come across this problem before.'

'Yes, you're right, as usual,' he smiled. However, as he spoke the words his thoughts were of a more sinister nature.

After a restless night and coffee for breakfast, he decided to take Evelyn's advice to see the man at We Vend Anything. While he waited for the salesman, he was ushered into a side room full of different types of machines, all with various upgrades. He winced as he saw the price tags. 'Must be joking,' he muttered.

'So, I believe you have been done,' said the smartly-dressed man as he entered.

'Done?'

'Yes, you know – your machines have been done over, broken into.'

'Yes, its bit of a sickener,' Derek said. 'I hadn't bargained on this. The money's all gone.'

'I'm afraid it is a common occurrence but don't worry. We have the answer.'

Derek smiled, but he was expecting the worst.

The man held out his arm and guided him towards the gleaming machines on the shelf. 'The Mark Two machines are impenetrable. They guarantee the security of your cash and the product. Unfortunately, because of the higher standard, they come with a premium price but peace of mind is assured and, compared to endless break-ins, it will work out cheaper in the long run. I'm sure you will agree that they do look more robust and secure.'

'So what have I got?'

'Ah, you have the Mark One machine. They're not exactly suited to insecure locations, more for a place where you can keep a permanent eye on them.'

'I can't do that! You never mentioned that when I bought them.'

'We didn't know at the time. Break-ins in this area are a new phenomenon.'

'Whatever. So it's going to cost me double what I paid in order to upgrade?'

'Afraid so, but it's all about peace of mind, isn't it?'

'So will you take back the machines that have been used?'

'No, unfortunately not. We don't deal in second-hand machines,' the salesman said sympathetically.

'Oh, come on! I paid good money for them and now you're telling me they're not up to it! I'm beginning to feel like I've been stitched up.'

'You may be able to sell them on the internet.'

'Aye, for a song.'

Derek was flabbergasted; he had bought the business, blown his ten grand, and now the company wanted to sell him upgraded machines at an extortionate price. He walked over to one of the Mark Two machines muttering, 'I should have known. The wife will kill me. Got to think fast.' He turned to the salesman. 'So what is the spec of these better, more secure machines? Have you got a catalogue?'

The salesman knew what Derek was up to, but had no choice. 'There you are. All the details are in there,' he said, handing over a glossy brochure.

Derek sat in his van and studied the enhanced security details of the Mark Two machines. At first he thought he could knock up something similar in his garage but the more he looked, the more he realised he wasn't up to it. He made a list of criteria from the brochure then, after getting clear in his mind what he needed, he set off to visit an old friend.

He hadn't seen this friend, Gregory, for a long time and thought it might be best to ring him first to make sure it was alright to call. 'Yes hi, I know it's been a long time, but I've got a proposition for you,' he said.

'Sounds interesting,' Gregory said. 'Call whenever you want.'

Derek went straight round and rang the bell. When he came to the door, Derek was shocked at his old friend's appearance. He was wearing shiny black boots and ex-army camouflage clothing, and his mop of thick black hair was replaced by a completely shiny bald head. 'Jesus, he must be expecting something serious to happen,' Derek thought.

'Come in,' Gregory said, as though his appearance was normal for the area.

Derek carried the vital part of the machine into the sitting room and placed it on the table.

Gregory ran his fingers over the neatly cut hole and nodded. 'Fuck's happened to this?' he said bluntly.

'Unfortunately, if I don't do something soon all my machines will look like this.'

'Really? Then you have a serious problem, especially if it's your living.'

'It is, so I have a proposition for you. You make these machines secure and I will give you a percentage of the takings until you are paid off.'

'OK, so far,' Gregory said.

Derek produced the catalogue from the company and opened it at the page displaying the upgraded machine and his handwritten criteria. 'This is what the company that makes them provide as an upgrade, but I can't afford it.'

Gregory adopted a sickly grin as he warmed to the proposition.' I see. When you say secure, are we at all interested in the welfare of the individual who is breaking into your machine?'

'Not at all.'

Derek's friend closed the brochure and slid it to one side. 'In that case, we have a wide and varied range of products at our disposal. I will give this my fullest attention and get back to you with suggestions within the next couple of days.'

'Brill,' said Derek.

Driving home, he felt more relaxed and positive that he had done the right thing. He was curious about the modifications Gregory would suggest, but decided to let them come as a surprise.

As he walked through the door, he wondered how much detail he should tell his wife.

'Hi...yes, a good day. Think I've sorted it.'

Yet another new plan

It had been a day or two since Digger and Spade chatted to Gillian in the cafe. Since then they had been busy trying to figure out the best use of her support, whilst keeping her from physical danger or potential job loss.

'If Gillian lost her job it might not be a bad thing. What a place to work in! It could be the motivation she needs. I'm sure she can do better than being in that office,' suggested Digger.

'Problem is, you usually find a job when you've got one. If she gets the sack, she'll be on the outside looking in. In other words, she won't be in control of her own destiny,' replied Spade

'That is very philosophical.'

'Personally, I think starvation is a great motivator. The smell of a bacon butty when you're skint can encourage the form-filling activity.'

'Yes, OK,' conceded Digger.

They had yet to establish a link between the man in the rubber suit and Granville, the owner of the company.

'There's got to be a link. One is a brain-dead nutter, the other is a power-crazed megalomaniac. They are probably mates,' uttered Spade as he unfastened his shoelaces. He was still following his doctor's instructions and resorted to bare feet whenever he could, but only when they were out of sight under the desk.

Digger, meanwhile, was on another track. 'Have you noticed that they've never been seen together?'

'Well, they wouldn't be; one is the boss and the other is a dipstick.'

'All we've seen is someone in a rubber suit. As for the owner, it's hearsay that he exists.'

'It's only a theory, but do you think the man in the rubber suit and the boss are the same person,' Spade asked.

'Ah, not mates, but very close. Close enough to morph into one! That's good thinking.'

'OK, sounds like a plan. Better update the board.' Spade rubbed out a section of text that was no longer relevant then inserted new notes. 'Find the man in the rubber suit,' he said as he wrote.

Digger looked troubled. 'Problem is, we are no nearer to finding the identity of the body parts. The people who we thought they belonged to have admittedly disappeared, but nobody seems to care. The man in the rubber suit that we are chasing is a side issue. We should be concentrating on eliminating those that work there and see who is left, then we might have names to work with.'

Spade nodded his head. 'OK, back to the board.' He rubbed out *Find the man in the rubber suit* and in its place wrote: *From list of employees, find out who has not been seen for a while.* 'There, my hand is aching now but it's a good plan. I'll get on to it.'

He went to the phone. 'Oh hello, it's DS Spade. We are investigating the missing persons at your factory. Do you think you could provide a list of personnel, their addresses and their job titles, please? I'll be round in an hour or so to pick it up.' He replaced the phone on its rest despite the angry protestations coming from the earpiece. 'That's that sorted. We could pick up your coat from the cleaners on the way. They should have stopped it smelling to high heaven by now,' he smirked.

Digger tilted his head. 'You can give them your socks in exchange.'

They arrived at the factory and parked in a visitor's bay. Almost as soon as they had switched off the engine, faces appeared at the office windows.

'Word has got around,' Spade said.

'Word has got around that they are now all suspects,' added Digger.

On this occasion they did not have to knock on the sliding window. The bespectacled secretary was waiting for them. 'I believe you have a document for us,' Spade suggested.

'Here,' she said, thrusting it though the hatch. She was just about to close the sliding door when Digger stopped her. He had witnessed the workforce on his recent nocturnal undercover visit and immediately noticed an error. He flicked through the list, mentally counting as he went. 'Erm, I'm sorry but this doesn't seem like anywhere near the number of people that work here.'

'There are a lot of individuals who work here who do not have a contract, so we don't know who they are.'

'I'm sorry, but this won't do. I need a list of *all* the people who have worked here in the past four weeks.'

The secretary hesitated then remarked, 'It's all we have. Like it or lump it.'

Digger smiled at Spade. 'Fine. If you like, I'll get inspectors in who will stop production, lock the gates and then do a roll-call. It's illegal to have people here when you don't know who they are. What happens if there is a fire or an incident?'

Panic set in. In the office many people picked up their phones.

'We will wait in this little room until you sort it,' Digger said.

As they walked towards the bugged room, Spade grabbed Digger's arm and pulled him back. 'This could be our opportunity to set a trap.'

Digger beamed at the prospect. 'We'll wind the bastard up and get him to show his face.'

They entered the bugged room and feigned small talk as they sat down.

'What you doing tonight?' Digger asked.

'Not much. Thought I'd watch a film or something.'

'Anyway, we should be home early now that we know what's going on here. I mean, the evidence is compelling. They've only recorded half the workforce and they say they don't know who the rest are. It's highly illegal and against health and safety, but they must have a list or a database somewhere. We'll need that to get a conviction and then the owner will be fined and the factory closed down.'

They sat in silence, pointing at the bugged phone and smiling as they waited for the secretary to return.

'This is an updated list of all the ones that we know about,' she said. 'They come by the bus load at night and go just as quickly. He gets them in just to finish an order off.'

Digger swiftly stood up, put a finger to his lips and pointed to the phone with his other hand. She realised what he meant and put her hands in the air. 'I hate it here,' she wailed as she left.

'That's another job lost. He'll have to bus in some secretaries next,' sniggered Spade, once they were outside of the factory.

'Or maybe we have another mole on the inside,' added Digger, tapping the side of his nose.

'Probably one who will rat on him.'

The banter flowed freely as they drove away, which was perhaps as well because they now had a list of employees that they didn't know what to do with, and had laid a trap for the boss and were unsure what to do if he fell into it.

'So, what do we do now?' asked Spade, as he scanned the list of names.

'What does it say about their job descriptions? Don't forget we are looking for the manager and the shop steward.'

'Everyone on here is a process worker, which could mean anything.'

Back at the office, Digger slipped out for a moment and immediately Spade reached for his mobile. 'Hi … it's me. Do you fancy going out for a pint?'

'What about your friend?'

'He's not my friend, he's just a work colleague and he won't mind…'

A knock-on effect

The upper floor of the We Vend Anything company had many offices, mostly occupied by telephone sales people whose daily occupation was to give an unsuspecting person the hard sell and convince them that they should invest their savings in the coin-slot vending industry. Their strategy was to give short shrift to the people who replied 'Thanks but no thanks', and concentrate on the 'Maybes'. To the telesales staff it was a numbers' game, and the objective was to get through as many numbers as they could.

In the centre of the sales floor was a sparsely furnished, glass-walled room with a large oval table. Normally this was used for educational purposes but, on this occasion, it was being used to communicate doom and gloom. A flickering fluorescent light appeared to emphasise the point.

The chairman stood at the opposite end to the personnel, seemingly distancing himself from any culpability, and immediately transmitted negative vibes. He had come from a meeting with the auditors and was instructed to 'cascade' disappointing financial details to his workforce. The unusually sombre tone in his voice told them all they needed to know.

He huffed and puffed as he switched on the OHP, then pointed with a stick. 'If we look at the line indicating income, it has spikes and troughs, profit and loss. We have analysed it and it refers to franchisees starting and leaving: profit when they get set up and loss when they leave. This is a big issue, because the overall trend is only just break even. In other words, if we don't watch it, we could easily go under. I see this as a managerial problem.'

He paused, then raised his voice. 'We are quite good at getting new franchisees to join but we cannot keep them. You are not looking after your men. They pay good money to join us but have no qualms in walking away. In fact, some franchisees literally dump the machines on our doorstep and run away. This cannot continue,' he said, pointing his stick at the men in crisp white shirts at the other end of the table.

There was a moment's deliberation as his words sank in, then a more outspoken member of the team stood up. 'Can I just say that this accusation is unfair and untrue? We support them as much as we can, but we are hampered by the extortionate price of the Mark Two machine. That is when they quit – they suffer a few break-ins, assess the situation, then go while they are still ahead financially. If the machines were cheaper we could guide them into buying them, but they are way too expensive.'

'We get them from the supplier. We are stuck with the cost of the bloody machines,' the chairman advised. He switched off the OHP, sat down, sighed and his aggression receded. 'Maybe we are looking at the problem from the wrong angle. The income is down because of the thefts, not because the Mark Two machines are too dear. We should be stopping the thefts,' he said with a hint of grit in his voice.

Eager to support his colleague, another member of staff bravely added his somewhat negative opinion. 'And how do you suggest we stop the thefts? You'll have us as security guards next.'

'If we don't do something, you might have to go and get yourself a job as a security guard.' The chairman looked round the room as if to say, 'Well, what's it to be?'

They nodded in resignation and he smiled again. 'That's better. Now, I want you to choose a rep who you think is having problems. Go and meet him, and for goodness' sake help him out.'

'How?'

'That's up to you,' he replied, walking through the doorway.

They sat in silence for a while before an unelected senior member of staff opened the discussion. 'Thing is, you can plot on a chart when the franchisees start and when they quit. Everyone is very enthusiastic at first, but as soon as they suffer a couple of thefts it knocks the stuffing out of them. They immediately start looking for something else. Somehow we have to support them before they get to that stage.'

A man who was doodling on his notepad offered an alternative strategy. 'I do like the softly-softly approach but I think it has gone beyond that. These opportunist thieves – because that's what they are – are looking for an easy hundred quid. They need to be made an example of. If word gets around that you can get your face rearranged if you so much as touch the machines, they'll think twice before robbing them.'

The intake of breath from the others was audible. There was another period of silence before another colleague had his say. 'One minute I'm a coin-slot instructor, the next I'm a hooligan. That makes me as bad as the thieves! But what if we got the owners together to form a kind of vigilante group so they could look after themselves? If they want to hire a thug, that's their business.'

There were smiles all round. Happy with the outcome, they each allocated themselves a name out of a hat.

***

'Derek? Hello, I'm John from We Vend. I believe there are security issues. I'm here to help. Can you come to a meeting?'

'All of a sudden help is a-plenty,' Derek replied cynically.

'Yeah, well, the company realises that you should not operate in isolation. If we can help in anyway, then so be it. Will you come?'

'No probs, I'll be there.'

'You're not going to believe this,' he said to his wife when he arrived home.

A meeting of minds

When Derek took on the coin-slot business, he'd assumed he would be working on his own, so he was pleasantly surprised to get the invitation to meet other vending-machine owners. As usual with this kind of trade, the meeting was at a hotel just off the motorway. When he arrived, he was amazed to find that he recognised others in the meeting. He had never considered that they also were in the coin-slot business. 'They must keep themselves to themselves, just like I do,' he thought.

He nodded and waved out of politeness then poured himself a complimentary coffee. The others responded and idle chit-chat ensued around the drinks' station.

A throaty cough brought the meeting to order and it opened with a curious request. 'After lots of deliberations we, the original members of the Coin-slot Operators Group, or COG for short, have decided that a clandestine approach to this gathering is preferable in light of recent happenings.'

'COG? Clandestine? Happenings? What's going on? I'm only a soap-mould filler,' muttered Derek under his breath.

'So from now on, names will not be used and each member will adopt a pseudonym appropriate to their vending product. For instance, I am Cuddly Toy Ken, and this is Chocolate Chip Charlie. So, if you could, please take a moment to come up with your alias. I know it is not easy but do your best.'

Derek's brain raced as he tried to think of a name. He decided to stall for time. 'Thank you for inviting me. I really do appreciate the support, even if it does feel like

I'm at a Masonic meeting. But what was this "happening" you mentioned?' Others followed suit and adopted facial expressions that indicated ignorance of the 'happening'.

Cuddly Toy Ken looked at each of them; they looked back, shaking their heads indicating a lack of knowledge of what he was on about. 'I thought it would have got around by now. The other night a thief was making his getaway when he was apprehended by another person who, without hesitation, stabbed him with a large knife.'

Gasps of shock went around the table and Cuddly Ken had to wait until the expressions of disbelief subsided.

'Aye, I know, bloody awful. It was caught on camera. Strangely enough, though, both persons fled the scene so the thief could not have been that badly hurt. Another peculiarity of the incident is that there was no evidence to suggest a stabbing other than the thief abandoning his booty. There were pound coins all over the car park – kids had a field day the following morning.'

'Bloody hell!' Derek exclaimed, still reeling from nature of the incident.

'It could have been any one of us!' announced Chocolate Chip Charlie.

The others, clearly shaken, went back to the coffee station for a top-up and a bourbon biscuit. As they sat down Derek posed a question. 'Who got stabbed? Was it the thief, the vendor or a member of the public?'

'Strange thing is, nobody seems to know. Both parties fled the scene and there are no witness reports, other than what was caught on the CCTV camera. I've not seen it myself but I talked to one of security guards who said it was a violent attack with a big knife.'

'Good grief,' affirmed another entrepreneur.

'Shocking, I know, but we are doing the right thing by forming a group.'

The others nodded approval and then there was a knock at the door. 'Come in,' Ken shouted.

'Well, well,' remarked Derek as he recognised the man who walked in.

'Hello, everybody. I know some of you but not all, so I will introduce myself. I am John from We Vend Anything and I have been asked by the company to provide support to your meeting and give any advice I can.'

'Got any cheap machines?' Derek sniped.

John looked at him, held up his palms but said nothing.

'Well I think it's very timely that the company is getting involved. It's their livelihood as well, you know. If we go down, they go down afterwards,' Charlie added thoughtfully.

'Thank you for that. Now, if you have sorted your names, we can carry on. If we can go round the table, ladies first...' Cuddly Ken said, reaffirming his role of chairman.

'Hello, everybody, can't think of a name – just call me Alice.'

'Yes, hello. I'm Stevedore. It's a play on words 'cos I have cranes.'

Ken looked at two other attendees who just shook their heads. 'OK, that's fine. Can I clarify the reason for this meeting? It is to somehow come up with a plan that will provide a deterrent to the growing problem of vandalism against our machines and our means of earning a living. I can only speak for myself, but I am getting increasingly angry about the situation and I would support any action to eradicate the problem.'

'Action?' queried Alice.

'Yes. I have found that direct action always works. Hit the bastards where it hurts, in the gob, if necessary. Naming and shaming will have no effect on this scum. We should *maim* and shame them.' Ken held up a fist to prove the point.

'I'm with you. I've lost too much putting these machines right. We should sort them out once and for all,' said Alice, standing up.

At this point the two others who couldn't think of names nodded to each other, stood up and walked to the door. 'Sorry,' one of them said, 'we didn't go into business to get involved like this. Aliases, maim or shame – not for us, thanks.'

'Oh dear, I'm sorry you feel this way,' Ken said sadly. 'Well, anyway, all the best.'

The meeting had not got off to a good start and the numbers were shrinking by the minute so Derek attempted to calm things down. 'Maybe maim and shame is a bit heavy. Personally, I think new technology should be employed. Apparently – or so I've been told –there are products on the market that could protect our machines remotely. The thief or perpetrator would be discouraged from breaking into your machine to a degree decided by you.'

The others were beginning to lose the thread of his argument. 'Sorry, not getting your drift. What do you mean by degrees?'

Derek tried to explain by listing the options his camouflage-dressed friend had related to him. 'Soft to hard, hard to extremely hard... You could put a notice on your machine that says "Please don't break into me", i.e. soft. Or "If you break into me you will get sprayed with irremovable dye", i.e. medium. Or hard, like "This machine is electrified and it will shock you if you fiddle with it". Or extremely hard – "This machine, if tampered with, will blow up in your face"...Or anything in between – cameras, alarms, sirens.'

The others smiled.

'Stuff the shame, I'm going for maim,' said Alice.

'Thank you for that,' Cuddly Ken said. 'So, back to the proposal. I would like to get a decision from the group – do we shame or maim these people? Those in favour of maim raise your hand… That's it, then. Unanimous!'

Ahhh, the friendly atmosphere of a coffee shop

Digger and Spade had arranged to meet Gillian for a chat in the café. Their intention was to lighten the atmosphere and not give out the heavy vibes of a police-station interview. Digger had thought long and hard about creating an alliance with a member of the public and, against his better judgement, he had decided to soften and mellow his approach.

'We want her on our side so, if we sit near the door, when she enters we can give her a cheery wave. It will calm her down, make her feel relaxed,' he said.

They tried the new method of greeting. Spade and a few other customers immediately felt it was way over the top; judging by the redness of Gillian's face, she was not best pleased. 'All my mates come in here and here I am on full view, sat with two strange men who are wearing long macs. What will they make of it?'

'Sorry, we can sit further at the back if you like,' Digger offered. 'Didn't want to cause offence, we just thought if we were near the door it would be easier for you to see us, that's all.'

'It's easier for all my mates to see us as well,' she hissed.

They picked up all the crockery and headed towards a more discreet table. There was silence for a moment to allow tempers to cool; all heads faced the wooden panelling, then slowly they returned to focus on their coffee. They adjusted their Columbian to individual taste and, after a sip, Digger spoke. 'It's like this. Has the owner been around? Only we left a message for him and we were wondering if he had responded or called in or anything.'

'Any phone calls, emails or any…mysterious happenings?' added Spade, trying to lighten the atmosphere by putting on a spooky voice.

Gillian ignored him and replied in a humourless tone. 'No, nothing. But the other day one lady said that the papers on her desk had been moved and a drawer left open. But she is getting forgetful – she could have done it herself.'

Digger smiled and rubbed his hands. 'It's like a game of chess. We move a rook, he moves a castle. We have to get him in a corner so he will lash out and expose himself.'

'Why don't you go and see him? He doesn't live that far away,' said Gillian, stating the obvious but in a less-clipped voice.

'No, we can't do that. We don't want to show our hand – our empty hand. We haven't really got anything on him, other than hearsay.'

'We want to catch him red-handed and exposed…so to speak,' Spade added.

'How about, red-faced, red-handed and exposed,' said Gillian, sitting back in her chair. She paused for effect then took a sip of her cooling coffee. Because of the lack of an enthusiastic response, she held a bourbon biscuit and slowly dipped it in her coffee to allow them more time to chew over her comment.

'Go on,' urged Spade.

'Apparently there are photos from way back. He was caught…*involved*…with one of his secretaries. She has long since passed away, so she won't be embarrassed any more, but in quiet moments in the office we point to the desk where it happened. It were nothing crude, just a passionate embrace at the Christmas party. This chap was going around with a camera, as they do, and pictures were taken without the boss knowing. Later, he went mad. It still makes us laugh. Got to be careful, though, you never know who is listening.'

'Do these photos exist?' queried Digger.

'Don't know. I've never seen them,' Gillian replied.

'Ah, but does *he* think they exist?'

'It doesn't matter if they don't exist, so long as he *thinks* they exist.'

'What is required is a coded message,' Digger suggested. 'We know he comes in late at night. Leave an empty envelope on a shelf with a note written on it that says *Photos of Christmas party* and the date you think it happened. Don't worry if you're a bit out with the date, he won't remember either. We are trying to prove that he is a serious control freak and, as such, would have known about the trouble in his factory. He could be involved in the mysterious disappearance of two members of staff.'

At which point the coffee had a diuretic effect on Digger's bladder and he hastily exited the table.

Gillian moved closer to Spade's chair. 'Does he know?' she asked. 'About us?'

'No, and there's no reason why he should.'

'What would happen if he found out?'

'Cross that bridge when we come to it.'

Digger returned, pulled up his chair, sat down, sighed and smiled.

'We were just saying, what would happen if the boss found out what we were doing and that he was the prime suspect?' said Spade.

'Oh, cross that bridge when we come to it,' Digger said.

More red faces and red hands

Derek sat glumly in his car. Things were not going according to plan. Firstly, he'd had another break-in to contend with. He'd thought the machine was in a vulnerable place, just slightly in an alcove, though not necessarily in the worst position. In light of the meeting with COG, he had taken tentative steps to protect his livelihood but, to his dismay, his theft-deterrent strategy had gone badly wrong.

As part of the least aggressive method to avert break-ins, he had installed a gadget inside the money container that sprayed an invisible dye over every coin that passed through the machine; in contact with the dye, the skin turned bright red. Unfortunately the warning notice meant to be read by potential thieves informing them of the effects of touching the coins had fallen off. As a consequence, this ever-so-slightly vulnerable machine had fallen victim to George's list of ones to be hit – and *had* been hit.

'Bugger, bugger, bugger,' Derek ranted, on finding the damaged machine.

But this was just the beginning. Immediately after the break-in, Derek rushed to the pub which, in his mind, was where thieves would go after committing a heist. He confronted the first man he saw who had red hands. 'Got you, you bastard!' he said gripping his arm.

'What the—?' the shocked man replied.

'Your hands, they're red! You must be the one who robbed my machine.'

Others in the pub, on hearing the accusation, went to the man's aid and held up their red hands. 'I am Spartacus,' they chanted together.

'The dye was supposed to highlight the thief but it has hit the whole town. Either that, or they must all be thieves,' he told Evelyn, who was holding her head in her red hands.

'This has not got to get out. We will be a laughing stock if people find out that you're responsible for all these people being red-handed. Do not mention it to anyone, do you hear?' she panicked.

'Don't worry, love, the dye wears off after a few days,' Derek replied, trying to calm her down.

'Whose idea was it anyway? You haven't told me about this. I could have told you this might happen.'

***

In another house indirectly connected to the effects of coming into contact with the invisible red dye, tensions were also rising.

'You do you know your hands are red?' Geoff's wife Ange asked, as the adverts distracted her from her round of the evening's soaps.

'I know. I've tried washing them but it won't go away,' Geoff replied, holding up his clean but red hands.

'Where's it come from?'

He hastily came up with a reason that he hoped would curtail the inquisition. 'I think I got it in the workshop. George has some funny stuff on his shelves. I've been using some stuff for degreasing machine parts...maybe it's that.'

'Well, whatever it is, you can't miss it. It's really bright. Hope it's not dangerous.'

Geoff had reverted to storing the cash in the garage. He lifted the lid on a tin; sure enough, as he lightly touched a coin with his index finger then held it up, it was glowing bright red. The hairs on the back of his head stood up as he recalled his journey back after his nocturnal activities.

Unfortunately for the inhabitants of Throttle, on the way home he had called into the twenty-four-hour supermarket to get some basics and unloaded a five-hundred-pound bag of coins into the machine that gave shopping tokens in return. Some of the coins from the token machine were bagged and went straight to the bank, but most ended up back at the checkouts and given out to shoppers in their change. Checkout personnel and shoppers were affected, to the delight of the local rag.

'Red-handed in Throttle' was emblazoned across the front page of following night's paper. It was reported that people all over town were affected and comparing redness had become a pastime.

It took a few days for the effects to subside. Some people said that repeatedly washing your hands in petrol reduced the glow. A footnote in the paper advised people not to do this whilst sitting in front of the fire.

In his garage, Geoff decided to try out the theory. Whilst wearing rubber gloves, he rinsed hundreds of coins in petrol then laid them out to dry. The fumes made his eyes water but he was reluctant to open the doors in case he was asked what he was doing. Finally, when he thought he was making headway, he stepped out into the garden for some fresh air.

As he inhaled deeply to clear his lungs, Ange approached carrying a basket of wet laundry. She had a cigarette between her lips and, being hindered from speaking, she politely nodded and a length of ash fell to the floor.

'No,' Geoff screamed, as he bundled her back into the house. 'You don't smoke while you're hanging out washing. You never know what might happen.'

A hastily arranged meeting of COG

The COG members sat silently around the table, arms folded and facial expressions that suggested more than mild irritation.

'Does anyone know?' asked Cuddly Ken silently.

'All the frigging town knows,' replied Chocolate Chip.

'I mean does anyone know where the dye came from?'

'They think it came from the supermarket.'

'That's good. Let them keep thinking that. So long as no one blabs, we will be OK.'

Chip did not agree. 'But the whole town is affected. Do you not see the seriousness of it? We could get locked up.'

'The fire brigade have been on high alert after a rumour that petrol gets rid of the dye.'

Ken did his best to calm things down. 'OK, so what happened? How come when the dye is only supposed to affect the robber it affects a whole town? We need to know?'

They nodded and turned to Derek. 'Well?'

'Hey, don't look at me. It's not my fault, I didn't rob my own machine and it wasn't me that put the coins into the supermarket. OK, I might have slightly overfilled the dye container – in fact I know I did – but how was I to know this would happen?'

A snigger that turned into a roaring laugh broke out among the others.

'Overfilled the container? The whole town is lit up at night by red hands.'

It took a while for decorum to return. After a moment of coughing and the wiping away of tears, it was back to 'any other business'. The silence was deafening because nobody raised their hand. Finally Ken leaned forward on the table and, in hushed tones, added his thoughts. 'The robber must be local. He has to be. He must have put some coins in the token machine on his way home.'

Derek sat back in his chair and sighed loudly in frustration; he looked around the room, took a deep breath and stated the facts as he saw them. 'After all this, we still don't know the identity of the robber. I'm two hundred quid down, plus the cost of the machine. The red dye will be gone in a couple of days and then it'll all be forgotten. The effects don't last that long and the newspaper will be used to wrap chips. I'm still out of pocket and we still don't know who did it.'

The others listened, each trying to find something to say but failing. Just as they thought he had finished, Derek took another breath and set off again. 'So what's next on the agenda? Do we throw our hands up in the air and quit, say goodbye to ten grand, throw the machines in the skip and trot off to the employment office? I don't know about you, but I have no option but to carry on. I can't say goodbye to ten grand. We have to find something that targets the person who is breaking in. I know it went wrong but at least I tried. We can't stop now.'

Gregory, Derek's camouflage-clad friend had accompanied him to the meeting and was listening intently; he had just finished a sleepless stint of watching a boxed set about a spy thriller. He had weighed up the situation and, to him, there seemed to be only one logical solution. He raised his hand and spoke. 'Nerve agent.'

'Nerve agent? Are you mad?' Cuddle Ken asked.

'Quite straightforward really, and cheap.'

'Go on.'

'It's simple. You paint a coin inside your machine that you never ever go near and that's it: thirty seconds after the robber lightly touches it, he's dead as a door nail. No more worries.'

'Apart from a stiff next to your machine and a life sentence, that is.'

'Only trying to help,' Gregory sniffed.

At the table Alice, who had been quiet throughout the meeting, threw in a comment that shut them all up and had them on the edge of their seats. 'There's a camera pointing down at the coin machine in the supermarket.'

There were smiles all around as a bit of sanity was introduced.

'Go on, tell us more,' the chairman urged.

'I work there at night filling shelves. I usually do the frozen-food section. I have to wear a fleece to keep me warm and put on gloves so my fingers don't get frostbite.'

Eyeballs rolled as she went on about bags of frozen peas and carrots. 'It's a hard job putting the food in its correct place. Anyway, where I work is at the top end, and the machine for the tokens is just the other side of the barrier, near the very last check-out. I was working there the other night and I noticed a camera right over it. If you want the identity of the robber, you should look at the video and see who exchanged a load of coins for tokens.'

Smiles turned to frowns as the enormity of the task of getting hold of the film became apparent; banter went round the table.

'So … get hold of the film, eh?'

'Be like mission impossible: "this message will self-destruct in ten seconds", mocked the man in the camouflage outfit.

'There's more chance of that than using a nerve agent,' Alice replied with feeling.

'They both seem a bit unachievable, if you ask me, not to mention illegal. And what happens if you get caught?'

'Don't worry, we will all come and visit you. Anyway, the video film – what's the feeling?' Ken asked.

'You can't just walk in and ask to see the film. It will be locked away by the security people and, if you do ask, they'll want to know what you want to see it for. Then the cat will be out of the bottle,' Alice warned.

'Cat...bag, genie...bottle. It's one or the other.'

'What?'

Not getting all your own way

Geoff was feeling more confident about his so-called career. His trips to the gym were paying off: he felt stronger, fitter and more able to handle the many and varied machines with ease. Since George had sorted out the interloper there had been no opposition, and Geoff found himself strutting about with an air of self-assurance that previously he would not have believed possible. He had got into a routine.

'Just like being at work,' he hummed, as he entered the premises of a large shopping centre. The simple items of equipment that he needed to gain access to the cash boxes were now neatly concealed about his person. This was much better than the early days, when he went out wearing the outfit that George insisted on, and he felt conspicuous and imagined that people were looking at the strange lumps and bumps in his jacket. He was amazed that there were certain retailers, usually on the internet, that supplied clothing for the very purpose of concealing thieving equipment. With a new suit that matched his newly acquired gait, Geoff felt the part.

About half an hour before closing was his target time for relieving the machines of their takings. The customers, or stragglers as he called them, would be on their way out and the staff were distracted by their preparations for the following day. They all let him get on with what he did to earn a living. If he was early, he could easily kill a bit of time window shopping.

On this occasion his timing was spot on. A quick look at the list provided by George indicated that three machines were highlighted. Experience had taught Geoff that three machines was the maximum for one visit from the point of view of getting rumbled; any more, and the weight of the coins became unmanageable.

He was on his way to the first machine on the list when he spotted an elderly gentleman standing a few feet away. He didn't look like he was going to use the machine; he was just standing there. The man looked grumpy. 'A lifetime of frowning,' Geoff thought.

The man was wearing a long dark overcoat that seemed to add to the weight of the shopping bags he had dumped on the floor. Geoff slowed down his pace to a casual saunter in the hope that the old chap would move on, but he remained. He looked suspiciously at Geoff then shuffled, but effectively stayed where he was.

Geoff looked at his watch; he decided that he could risk an extra couple of minutes, so went to look at a few shop windows. After ogling and gasping at the price of expensive leather brogues and commenting, 'When will I be able to afford shoes like that? Probably never,' he looked at his watch again. Time was getting on and this delay would put his routine out of sync.

The old man wasn't for moving, so Geoff asserted himself and approached slowly. He nodded and the man half-heartedly gestured in return. Geoff stood in front of the machine but he was almost touching the gentleman. He waved his arms as an indicator that space was an issue, but either the man did not understand Geoff's vibes or he was being stubborn.

'Er, excuse me, sir. Could you give me a bit of space whilst I service this machine? A bit of elbow room, if you will.' Geoff smiled in an attempt to lighten the situation, but to no avail.

The man huffed and moved one pace away then shuffled again.

'I won't be long,' said Geoff, as he reached inside his jacket for his power unit.

The elderly man watched with interest as Geoff swiftly cut the hole and inserted his scoop to retrieve the coins. There was a pause. Geoff turned and their eyes met. For a moment they glared at each other then, realising what he was witnessing, the man raised the alarm. 'You're not servicing it, you're breaking into it! Security! Help! He's robbing the machine,' he shouted.

Geoff's mood changed and he felt himself boiling over. 'Fuck off, old man,' he said, holding up the power unit and stepping towards him.

The man grabbed his bags and cowered as Geoff approached. He had been waiting for his wife who was having some retail therapy; luckily, she came out of a shop opposite and observed the incident. 'Come away,' she screamed at her husband.

'He's breaking into the machine and now he's going to hit me with a drill!' the old man shouted, loud enough for all the remaining shoppers to hear.

'Come away! Don't get involved,' his wife shouted, pulling him by the arm.

'It's good advice, old man, now fuck off,' Geoff said, still holding the power unit aloft.

The couple set off down the mall with the man still protesting at his wife's insistence that they should leave. 'He's a robber! They shouldn't be allowed to get away with it,' he ranted.

When they were at a safe distance, though still within earshot of Geoff, his wife concurred with her husband's theory. 'OK, we find a big burly security man and let him deal with the robber,' she said as a warning for Geoff to hear. The pair nodded, smiled at each other, then made for the exit waving and shouting.

Geoff watched, listened and panicked. He dropped most of the coins on the floor as he fled the building. In his haste, he bumped through the large plate-glass doors. People shouted as he pushed past them, not caring if he bundled them to the floor.

'He's a robber, stop him!' one yelled.

Geoff didn't turn round to see if he had hurt anyone, he just threw his tools on to the passenger seat of his car and slammed the driver's door. He looked across the car park and spotted uniformed men heading his way. The ignition key danced in his fingers as he attempted to insert it in the slot; the old car burst into life and, in a cloud of smoke from spinning tyres, he sped off towards the barrier.

He had to tailgate another car that was exiting and, in his urgency, pushed the car through bumper to bumper. The driver of the car in front held his hand on the horn as he was pushed out of the way, then waved his fist at Geoff who raced past, one hand on the steering wheel and one hand over his face to shield his identity.

Once out of the shopping estate, he slowed down to a normal speed while continuously glancing into his rear-view mirror. When he was sure nobody was following, he turned into side street, parked up and switched off the engine. He was drenched in sweat and trembling. He tilted the mirror to check his appearance.

'Would I have hit him? I was heading that way – only good luck his wife came out when she did, otherwise I might have... What then, for fuck's sake?' In his mind's eye, Geoff visualised the man lying on the floor with a pool of blood forming around him.

He sat pondering what could have happened until his sweat went cold. 'Better keep this to myself. George won't like it, but I can't go back. They will all know me now.'

He drove to a pub close to home and considered the excuses he could use for the day's lack of takings. 'Fuck it, I'll just say I was sick. I didn't go out 'cos I was sick. Everybody is allowed to have a sick day.' And with that, he smiled to himself and went inside for a pint.

He stood at the bar, savouring the freshly-tapped real ale. He wondered if he would ever meet the old man and his wife again. 'It's not that far away. Would they recognise me?'

Resting his pint, he speculated at the possibilities. 'Cameras, security guards, shoppers – it was only fleeting but I bumped into them all. I'll have to think of a reason for George, 'cos there's no way I can go there again. All that money left on the floor. I suppose the old couple will be writing out a statement about now, telling security how I threatened to hit him.'

At that moment he felt a shudder go through his body. 'I bet it will be in the newspaper: "Elderly couple doing their shopping threatened by a yob, white male, five feet ten smartly dressed. Reward offered". Oh fuck.'

A man he used to work with recognised him and patted him on the shoulder. 'Hello, Geoff, not seen you for a while. What have you been up to?'

Geoff held up his hands, put them to his mouth then raced to the gents and threw up.

An extra-extraordinary meeting

The remaining members of COG gathered in the large foyer of a motorway hotel. As predicted, mid-morning was very busy. 'There won't be any seats because of all the bloody salesmen using it as an office,' muttered Cuddly Ken.

The many charger leads strewn across the floor confirmed that he was right. The noisy clacking of laptop keypads and the unnecessarily loud discussions on mobile phones dissuaded the COG members from sitting nearby so, after grabbing a coffee, they moved to a conservatory and sat amid the leafy plants and water features. They squeezed around a table made from wooden pallets.

As he put down his paper cup, Ken turned to Alice and pointed at the rustic furniture. 'Bit rough, aren't they? Not my idea of furniture. Times must be really hard – you find these all over the place these days. It's weird, they cost a fortune in the shops but builders' skips are full of them. They throw them away.' He laughed hoarsely.

'I've seen complete sets of garden furniture made from them. I think it's meant to be minimalist,' she added, only touching the surface lightly to avoid getting splinters.

Derek was seething; he tried eyeballing the others in an effort to get the discussion underway but failed. He was the one who had called the meeting and now it had been hijacked by a conversation about wooden pallets and the many things you could make from them. He drummed his fingers on the rough-sawn wooden table top then stood up. 'Can I bring this meeting to order? I know you have got better things to do but there's been another robbery, and this time it was in broad daylight. We have to do something,' he pleaded.

The others listened intently. Chocolate Chip tried to sympathise, but didn't really help. 'We are sorry, but I don't see what we can do. Why don't you put some more money into it – get better machines? Accept the robberies as part of the game.'

Unfortunately for Derek, most of the others nodded in agreement.

'I can't afford it, otherwise I would. Do you know how much those Mark Two machines are?' Derek protested.

Ken added what the others were thinking. 'Look, we know they're not cheap but what else can you do? And, if you ask me, anything beyond that is too scary. I'm afraid I need to sleep at night.'

Several of the members pushed back their chairs in an attempt to leave until Alice, who was still admiring the furniture, uttered a curious comment. 'Sleeping is good for you, you should try it. Camomile tea before you go to bed. Wonderful.'

'I haven't slept for weeks and I think it will take more than camomile tea to sort, but thanks anyway.' Derek thought for a moment longer then ignored her advice. He could see he was fighting a losing battle but carried on. 'We have to up the game. We can't let them get away with it – this is our livelihood.'

Derek's camouflage-clad friend Gregory had come along for the ride and was itching to offer advice. He raised his hand and waited. Conveniently, there was a pause as the others ruminated about what else could they do. 'Can I offer a suggestion?'

Anticipating Gregory's train of thought, Ken butted in. 'If it's anything lethal, toxic or limb-removing, count me out.'

'Hey, there's no need for that. I'm only here in an advisory capacity. But it will come, trust me. These people don't understand reasoned discussion; they are thieves who see other people's money as fair game. They don't care about your property or how much you've invested, they just take it.'

Derek's frustration boiled over. He stood up and thumped the table to let the others know where he stood. 'He's right! We have to make a stand. If we make an example of one of them, they'll soon stop. If we...'

'If we what? Harm them?' Cuddly Ken demanded.

'No, no, what I mean is if we hurt them a bit...just a little bit.'

Within minutes, the membership had been reduced to just Derek, John from the company and Ken the chairman.

'Are we still quorate?' Ken asked.

'Does it matter?' asked Gregory, who wasn't sure what quorate meant.

Derek was not downhearted by the reduction in members so threw open the discussion. 'We tried the fluorescent red paint. It did not go as planned, I grant you, but we do know that it worked – too well, really. The whole town knows that it worked. But on that basis we know that the perpetrator was covered in it and, as such, he must know that we are not going to let this situation carry on. So what's next, Gregory?' As he finished his sentence he turned to face his friend. 'Sorry, I didn't mean to out you like that.'

'So my anonymity is blown. No problem.' Gregory reached into his pocket and produced a small battery-shaped electrical component. He placed it on the table with the two shiny terminals facing upwards. 'Do not touch the terminals. I will repeat that for those who were asleep: under no circumstances do you touch the terminals. OK?' he said grimly but with feeling.

The others nodded then sat back.

'What is it?' enquired Derek.

'This is a capacitor. It's like a battery but whereas a battery discharges its current in a steady and controlled manner, this does it instantly. Whack!! All in one go.'

The others in the group, and several other occupants of the conservatory who had started to earwig the conversation, jumped back when Gregory shouted 'Whack!'

'You really are mad, you know. You do know that, don't you?' suggested John.

Gregory, not to be dissuaded, carried on with his lesson in maiming people. 'As the thief breaks into the machine, it triggers this to become live. Then, as he pokes around inside for the cash, whack!!' he shouted again.

'Now I know you are mad.'

'It's not lethal, but it will make your tongue go fat. It's about ten thousand volts. If the thief gets a shock once, he won't want another.' Gregory laughed menacingly.

Derek liked the idea and smiled for the first time in ages. 'Not lethal but eye-popping... Sounds good to me. But how do you prevent me from getting a belt?'

'Well, first off, if the machine hasn't been broken into it shouldn't be live. But just in case, there is a switch hidden inside the case. But the best part is the cost – only a fiver off the internet. There will be vulnerable machines, so try a capacitor in one of those. For a fiver it makes economic sense.'

John, the company representative, appeared edgy. 'I've come here because the company is – how shall we say – not making as much money as it should. As a result of the robberies, it has become unattractive as a business model. So I'm here to help, but I'm not sure I can get involved in electrocuting people.'

'Ah, but if the temporary measure of the un-lethal capacitor deters the thief, and it gets around the criminal fraternity that it isn't worth the risk of breaking into the machines any more, then the franchise reverts to being a sound commercial investment,' Derek explained. 'And if you were the man who'd spearheaded the resurgence in the company's fortunes, wouldn't that make you a major candidate for promotion? Yes?'

John offered a thin smile and a hesitant nod. 'Suppose so.'

'Good,' said Derek

Gregory picked up the capacitor and spun it in the air before catching it and returning it to his pocket. Chairs were knocked over and coffee was spilt as they all sought safety. Gregory laughed. 'You don't think I'd be daft enough to bring a charged one in, do you?'

As they straightened up the chairs, hollow laughs could be heard. 'Course we didn't.'

Another waiting game

Inside his workshop, George slid the security bolt on the small external door. Even though he rarely had visitors, he didn't want to be explaining exactly what was doing this late at night to any bored security guard who just happened to be passing by and was curious about the lights inside.

George had given Geoff the list of machines to be emptied and explained any peculiarities. When he was sure that all was OK and Geoff had set off, he could relax and take it easy.

Being methodical, he immediately approached a large planner fixed to the wall. It contained a database in coded numbers of all the machines they'd raided, their location and the date last visited. The index to the coded numbers was in George's head, and there was a back-up on the hard drive of the computer. He was fascinated by numbers and formulas, and used the constant referencing to various locations and sites to keep his brain functioning, a game he played every day.

He found the block on the chart relating to this evening's exploit, rubbed out the existing date and inserted today's date with his felt-tipped marker pen. He could have done this on his computer but he liked the idea of being able to observe the data in one go.

He was about to start tidying up when there was a faint knock at the door. He turned, wondering if he was hearing things, then he heard it again. He was secretive about his activities; very few people knew what he did for a living or where he did it, so this was a mystery.

Curiosity eventually got the better of him and he walked cautiously to the door. He listened for any clues as to the identity of the visitor then carefully slid back the bolt and opened the door slowly to avoid its customary squeak.

'Hello, George,' said Geoff's wife.

'Angela! How can I help you?' he asked, taken aback that she would visit him on her own at this hour of the night.

'Firstly, you can invite me in. It's a bit cold out here,' she said with a certain forwardness that surprised him.

George stumbled over his words. This was unlike him; he could handle most circumstances but he felt on the defensive. He peered across the car park then looked at the clear night sky. 'You're right, it is a bit cold... Well... OK, I suppose so. You better come in.'

Being paranoid, he let her in then looked left and right out of habit before bolting the door. Ange smiled at his behaviour and entered the dimly-lit workshop; the only illumination came from the lights shining from the office windows.

She put two and two together. 'Not doing any repairs tonight?' she asked, as she edged towards the office.

'No, not tonight,' he said bluntly.

'Do you do many repairs?' she pried further.

'When required...when required.'

'He's not a good liar, our Geoff. He hasn't actually said what you do, but then he hasn't actually said what *he* does. But I know he doesn't get his hands dirty, other than by handling pound coins.'

'They do get surprisingly dirty,' George responded guardedly. 'Could be he's just a clean worker. I do advise the wearing of gloves and barrier cream.'

She smiled a cheeky grin at him, indicating a lack of sincerity on his part. 'Oh, come on, George. Our Geoff doesn't know one end of a spanner from the other, so the idea of him as a maintenance man… And he's a mucky worker. You should see the state of the house, the garden, not to mention the garage. We can't move for rubbish. And, as far as the use of barrier cream – our Geoff? Not a hope.'

'He works fine with me. I've no complaints.'

As he spoke, she scanned the gloomy workshop. 'Nothing has changed. It's just like last time. Same machines.'

'Things don't have to change to move on. Come on, what is it you're after?'

'I just need to be part of it,' Ange said. 'I'm bored, I need a purpose.'

'Part of what? There's nowt to do here, only wait.'

She spotted the large database on the wall and moved closer to have a look. 'I could help you fill this in,' she added, as she let her finger follow the horizontal line until she found today's date. 'Is this where he is tonight? Ten machines? We'll be rolling in it.'

George started to lose his temper. 'Enough! I fill in this chart and it's none of your business what I do.'

'But it is… Don't get angry, I'm just interested in what Geoff does and where the money comes from.'

There was a pause as George gathered his thoughts and took a deep breath. 'Now look,' he said, calming down. 'I do the research about the machines, that's why only I can fill in the chart. I pass the info to Geoff and two hours later he comes back with the money from the machines. In the meantime, we wait.'

'Then while we wait, I'll make you a brew.' As she filled the kettle from a tap in the workshop, Ange glanced across to the chart of many numbers.

'You'll have to go before your husband comes back,' George warned.

'I can help you fill in your chart. I can't figure out where these places are but the rest seems straightforward enough.'

'Really? A right little clever clogs.'

'But if you tell me what to write, that would be OK, wouldn't it?' She smiled and switched on the kettle.

'How does Geoff put up with you?' George asked.

A plan B

Digger and Spade were lost in their own thoughts. Sitting at their desks, both had got the detective's equivalent of writer's block.

Digger looked up from a form he was filling in and threw out a metaphorical sprat. 'From the demonstration the other day, I gather you weren't that good at cricket. You missed the door by miles.' There was a pause; he smiled as he watched his colleague shuffle in his seat and his ears prick up. 'How are you at five-a-side?'

Spade stared at him with a suspicious frown. 'Not sure I like the way this is going. Why do you ask? Come on, spit it out?'

'You know we have to crack this case before it is snatched away and given to some other eager, promotion-chasing backstabber. Yes?'

'Yes, but what's that got to do with me and five-a-side? And in any case, I reckon I could have hit the door every time after a bit of practice.'

'I'm coming to that. But don't you agree that if we don't do something soon, we could end up behind a desk, licking and sticking envelopes?'

'It had crossed my mind but evidence is a bit thin at the present.'

'Ah, well… In order to expedite matters, I think we need someone on the inside of the factory to find out what is going on. Preferably someone who can play five-a-side.'

'Really?' replied Spade, showing zero enthusiasm.

'Really. And what's more, I think it's such a good plan that I've already got it OK'd from above and been in touch with Gillian, who says she can get you on the pay role so that it looks kosher,' Digger said triumphantly.

'I still don't understand how five-a-side comes into this "good plan".'

'Last time we were there, I saw a poster asking people who worked there to join the five-a-side team. You would fit in right away, athletic-looking guy like you. Then, while chatting about football, you can keep your ear to the ground... Easy.'

'I'm crap at football,' Spade said morosely.

'That's good – you'll have lots to talk about. Now go home and get some kip. You start on the night shift tomorrow.'

'What? I had plans. I'm going out tomorrow.'

'Cancel them. This is important.'

Trying to go to sleep when he was not tired was difficult for Spade. As a consequence, the couple of hours he did get meant he did not sleep later during the night. Luckily he saw his haggard-looking, baggy-eyed appearance as a positive. 'They will all look like this,' he thought as he faced the mirror.

He decided not to shower or shave and selected his clothing from the wash basket in order to fit in. 'Body odour and stubble. How much of a disguise should I need?' he asked, whilst selecting a pair of well-used socks.

As arranged, Spade turned up at the factory entrance. He adopted a casual gait, that of the unwashed and unemployed, he thought. A ventilator high up on the wall belched out what he hoped was steam but the acidic stench hit him right way; he coughed and wondered how he would survive the shift.

'Harry? Is it Harry? I'm Alf. Come on, get a move on or we'll be late.' A man of similar age beckoned him whilst holding open the door to the factory.

Spade had read the introductory letter in his back pocket but, in the heat of the moment, had forgotten his new name. 'Harry, yes Harry. Oh God,' he thought.

Urging him on, his new colleague ushered him to his work area. 'We're in the packing department. You're working with me tonight till you get the hang of it.'

As they rushed past the production line, Spade spotted the five-a-side notice and paused. 'I owe you for this, Digger,' he muttered.

'Do you play five-a-side?' asked Alf, spotting him reading the poster.

'Don't you start,' went through Spade's mind. Then he spoke aloud. 'Occasionally. When I do play, I prefer to stay on the wing sending in accurate crosses.'

Alf gazed at him, surprised; he hadn't expected such a clipped and intelligent reply. 'Jesus, Harry, you sound posh. Where are you from?'

Realising his slip-up with his accent, Spade quickly adjusted. 'Sorry, only taking the piss. I'm crap really.'

This exaggeration did not impress Alf at all. He sighed. 'Weird,' he said as they stood either side of the as yet empty but moving conveyor belt.

The noise of the machine took Spade by surprise and instinctively he put his hands up to his head. 'How do you cope with this?'

'Oh, you get used to it. It doesn't bother you after a while.'

'You mean you go deaf.'

Alf was becoming aware of Spade's peculiarities and assumed he was being a clever dick so ignored him. 'OK, our job is to inspect the boxes as they go past and ensure that they are full. If they're not, you top them up from the boxes by your side.'

'Seems easy enough. What else do we do?'

'Trust me, that's enough.'

Moments later a shrill whistle blew; the conveyor speeded up and boxes headed towards them. Spade was expecting to see boxes with just the odd item missing but he looked across to see Alf's hands become a blur as he topped up the partially full cartons.

'Come on, I can't do it on my own,' he shouted above the din of the machine.

'OK, I'm doing my best but it's too fast,' Spade protested.

As the shift moved on and production settled down, the boxes were less likely to need topping up. Although they dared not look up, conversation was possible between the two men.

'How do you keep it up?' Spade asked. 'We've only been going half an hour and I'm knackered already.'

'It's not so bad, once you get used to it. You switch off and plan your day, or dream of sleep – wonderful deep sleep. I don't think my body has adjusted to night shift. I'm still sleeping at the wrong time of the day. It can't be good for you. When I'm in the pub, everyone's having a good time and I'm yawning my head off.'

'Do people nod off on the production line?' Spade's asked casually.

Alf looked at him with a fixed stare but did not reply. Luckily a series of half-full boxes approached and complete attention was needed to accomplish their task. It also provided thinking time for Spade's new workmate. 'Fancy a game of five-a-side, do you?' he asked, having regained his sociability

'If you think I'm good enough.'

They continued topping up boxes then Spade noticed that Alf was distracted.

'Who's this?' a voice from behind asked.

Spade turned; a large gentleman in a white smock held a clipboard and was running his finger down a list of names.

'It's Harry,' said Alf, trying to be helpful.

'That's right, I'm Harry,' Spade said.

'Surname?' the man demanded.

Spade quickly took the letter from his back pocket; as he passed it over, he scanned the name on the top. 'Harry, Harry Jones,' he repeated.

'Have to look on a letter for your name, do you?'

'No, you just took me by surprise, that's all.'

'Well, you're not on my list. What agency have you come from?' the white-smocked man continued as he wrote the name Harry Jones at the foot of the list.

'Oh, no agency. I just heard they were short-handed so I knocked on the door. A lady gave me the letter and said turn up for the shift, so here I am.'

'Not really the correct procedure but I don't suppose it matters as we need a replacement. You'll have to buck up, though. There are boxes with missing contents all over the place.'

'Yes, sir...replacement,' responded Spade, holding out his hand and hoping to be introduced.

'On your bleeding bike,' the man grunted as he turned and walked away.

The shift rattled on and began to take its toll on Spade. His hands hurt from grabbing the produce and his back ached from leaning over the conveyor belt. Standing upright, he stretched his back then flexed his hands to ease the pain. 'Do we get a break?' he shouted across the conveyor belt.

'Not officially,' Alf mouthed, as though it were a secret.

'Not officially? What do you mean?'

Alf looked up and pointed at the clock, then nodded towards a pallet full of boxes. Miraculously, the conveyor slowed down and shuddered to a halt; a cloud of steam belched from behind the machinery – it resembled a monster.

The workers hastily left through a side door to get away from the heat and noise. Spade and Alf followed. 'So this is the unofficial break?' Spade surmised.

His friend hushed him and they walked to one side. 'The bonus is paid on quantity by the hour. We've achieved that, so there's no point producing any more, not till we are well into the next period.'

Spade was listening intently until he spotted the man in the rubber suit through the open door. 'Who the hell's that?'

Alf turned and just caught the rear of the suited man as he trundled off down the walkway. 'He's the man who runs the joint. Whatever you do, don't argue with him. He is so scary.'

Spade touched the side of his nose to agree. After thirty minutes or so, they drifted back in and took up their positions alongside the conveyor belt.

After the end of the shift, Spade rang the office to report in. 'Half an hour on, half an hour off, all night... We could have produced twice as much,' he said to Digger, who had come in early to take his call. 'And guess who's in charge? That's right, the man in the rubber suit. He controls everything. Bloody hell, is he terrifying. I wouldn't like to cross him – everyone is shit scared of him.'

'That's excellent! I feel like we're getting somewhere. You're doing a grand job.'

'So how long?'

'How long what?'

There was a pause and an audible sigh from Spade. 'How long have I got to keep this up? I'm not sure I can keep the pretence going for much longer. I've nearly dropped myself in it twice. Soon they will smell a rat and, by the look of them, they don't take prisoners.'

Digger sympathised but he was caught between two stools. He didn't want Spade to get hurt, but it did appear that Spade was getting closer to vital clues in this investigation. To quit now would be premature. 'The idea of this ruse is to gain information in order to solve the mystery of the two bodies. There have not been reports of any locals missing, so it looks like it's somebody from out of town.'

'Replacement,' said Spade, his tone sombre.

'What?'

'They said I was the replacement, but replacement for who?'

'There you have it,' Digger said with elation. 'Find out who you are replacing and why. Then it's out of there and off to the pub.' He could hear Spade yawning over the phone. 'OK, go get some sleep so that you'll be alert for the next shift. Bye bye.'

This time Spade nodded off as soon as his head hit the pillow. Now it was his turn to dream about the man in the rubber suit.

Opportunists come in various sizes

There is a community that views life from a different perspective to ordinary people. To the everyday person, this particular community is abhorrent, though it probably comes as no surprise that there are certain individuals who do not strive to achieve by normal means riches, or even just a basic living. Members of this community do not feel the need to go to educational establishments to gain skills or qualifications that would give them employable status. In fact, they see this route to earning a living as a waste and certainly wouldn't dream of a four-year university degree course, or creating a CV, or any of the other paraphernalia that accompanies obtaining a job. The word 'job' does not appear on their list of boxes to tick or, for that matter, in their vocabulary. They live in an underworld where local and national news has no bearing whatsoever, where other people's problems are other people's problems; they couldn't care less about environmental issues or the state of the planet. They live for today and what they can easily nick.

Joe and his shorter friend, Arnold, belonged to this alternative community; they were thieves and very proud of it. As robber journeymen they strived to be the best and fitness was the key. So they practised sprinting and leaping over stooping pensioners or garden fences to facilitate a quick getaway, whilst at the same time pulling forward their hoods to conceal their identity. This was a complicated manoeuvre and required hours of training to achieve a seamless action. Alertness was vital to any business, and imperative if they were to avoid being caught, so sleep was cherished. Rise and shine before ten was frowned upon and this seemed to suit them perfectly.

'But,' as Joe lectured Arnold, 'we are different because we do not pre-plan our outings. And the reason we do not pre-plan is because we are opportunists.'

Arnold was drifting away; he hadn't understood a word Joe had said other than the fact that apparently they did not pre-plan. Whether that was good or bad, Arnold wasn't sure. 'If we don't have a plan, then maybe we should get one,' he said, trying to be involved.

'No, pre-planning means going out repeatedly to commit a crime in a certain way. But we are not like that, we do not have a pre-planned method that we repeat over and over again. Some criminals have been apprehended because they've been identified by their particular pre-planned method. We adapt to our surroundings and take opportunities as they come along. We are opportunists and, as such, in theory we have a better chance of getting our hands on other people's assets and, more importantly, a greater chance of getting away with it... Get it?'

Arnold still didn't get it but, to keep the peace, was prepared to accept whatever Joe said.

As they prepared to go out on their daily round, they compared the various accessories they needed. 'I saw a great hoody top the other day. You can pull it right over your head and it's got goggles built into it. It's used by the army for bad weather but it's cracking for robbing in,' enthused Joe.

'Seen this?' said Arnold pulling out a floral-decorated shopping bag. 'It folds up to nothing, then into its own bag. How cool is that?' he added, demonstrating how it worked.

Joe wasn't convinced. 'So they can't see your face but they recognise you by your gaudily-decorated shopping bag.'

Arnold wasn't going to be put off. He shrugged his shoulders and stuffed the now-tiny bag into his large shoplifter's pocket.

They set off happily, wondering what would come their way but firm in the knowledge that, whatever it was, they could handle it.

Recently, motorway services had developed into shopping malls with products of all kinds spilling into the aisles. For opportunist thieves this provided endless ways to fill their bags. They would stand on the edge of motorway service-station car parks and wait for coaches disgorging travellers who were either heading towards the café or the toilets. In order to get there, the travellers encountered the mountain of goods for sale. Joe and Arnold would mingle with them, filling their swag bags as they made their way down the mall. Afterwards the weary travellers would return from the washroom and be surrounded again by the goods for sale, totally unaware that they were providing the shoplifters with excellent cover.

'A coach every ten minutes. We'll need a big van at this rate,' said Joe confidently. As he spoke, another opportunity caught his eye. In the side of the glistening, chrome-plated vending machine was a dark gaping hole. This was not as it should be, and he knew right away that it had already been robbed. Experience told him that these machine robbers moved quickly and invariably left cash behind, so curiosity insisted that he should investigate further. Fortunately for the previous robber of the machine, he had used a plastic scoop to empty the cash box; he was not aware that this ten-pence plastic implement had saved him from horrific suffering, not to mention eventual arrest.

Unfortunately for Joe the opportunist, the second thief in this saga, he could only see one goal: scavenging the remaining pound coins that had been left behind by the previous thief who had hastily vacated the scene of the crime. 'Come on, this is for us,' he said with glee to Arnold.

Joe warily approached the vending machine so as not to raise attention, stooped down and peered into the cash box. Grinning, he looked at his colleague. 'There must be fifty quid in there. Here, hold out the bag,' he instructed.

Arnold looked around then opened the neck of the floral shopping bag. Joe put one hand on top of the machine to steady himself then gently but firmly forced his hand deep into the machine. He winced as he felt the components cutting into him, but he was determined not to leave without the pickings.

He thrust further and deeper into the mechanism until, unbeknown to him, the back of his hand lightly touched the exposed electrodes of the now-activated capacitor. If machines have feelings, and let's say this one was upset at being described as vulnerable, plus it was vexed at being violated by a common thief, it is understandable why it vented its anger onto the hand of the intruder.

A sudden shock raced up Joe's arm and shook his whole body; his hand was now firmly trapped in the mechanism and felt like it was on fire. Actually, it was. On its route from one terminal to the other, the electric current flashed across the back of Joe's hand; at the same time there was a loud crackle, a bright light flashed, and a dense plume of smoke oozed up to the ceiling of the mall.

Joe was in an uncontrolled muscular fit; his eyes bulged and rolled back, his mouth widened and his tongue flapped like a flag in a high wind. The screams he emitted were loud and bloodcurdling. The more he tried to pull out his hand, the more the mechanism cut into him and the louder he wailed. In an effort to free himself, he backed away and tipped over the stand supporting the machine. People stood transfixed as he fought to release himself.

Joe and the machine writhed on the floor like wrestlers in a ring. Finally he removed his mangled hand and backed away, cradling his bleeding fingers. The atmosphere was now full of the stench of burning flesh; customers, who approached to see what was going on, held their noses and backed away.

The route to the cash box was now free and, as it rolled to its resting place, it spilled out the remaining coins. This final movement was not lost on Arnold. He watched Joe receiving the full attention of the gathering crowd then, following the opportunist thief's guiding principle, he hastily gathered up the money, stuffed it into his bag and ran down the mall to the exit.

'I'll split it with you when we get home,' he shouted, not knowing if Joe heard or not. Once outside, he held open the floral bag and crudely estimated the value of the haul. 'Bit more than fifty quid, not bad for ten minutes work.'

Back in the mall, questions were being asked but Joe remained silent, apart from the odd yelp as he tried to move. Several security men arrived but, after a short discussion, it was decided that medical assistance should come first.

A first aider, who was short of practice, welcomed the chance to put his training into use. Having donned a white smock and carrying a large box with a red cross on it, he raced to the scene and announced his arrival. 'Coming through... Let me attend to the casualty,' he said, snapping on new protective latex-rubber gloves.

He held Joe's hand and assessed the lacerations and burns. 'Bloody hell, you've made a right mess of this. What were you thinking of, sticking your hand in an electric machine?' he commiserated as he dabbed the leaking fingers with a surgical swab.

Joe did not reply.

'No electric on these,' advised a trader, who knew the workings of vending machines and was fully aware of what Joe had been doing. He showed little sympathy and urged the first aider to ask further questions. 'Go on, ask him again what he was doing sticking his hand in the machine.'

With his uninjured hand, Joe pointed towards his gaping mouth and beckoned the first aider to come closer. To avoid catching anything nasty, the first aider put his ear to Joe's mouth but still at a far enough distance away that he thought viral infections could not be transmitted. He listened intently to Joe's mumbling then related the response. 'He can't say any more. He says his tongue has gone fat.'

Heard it on the grapevine

News of the occurrence spread quickly through the network of traders and a hurriedly arranged conference call between the remaining members of COG got underway. The gory details were greeted with a mixed reaction.

'Well, if you ask me it was a rip-roaring success,' said Gregory, who had now been co-opted as a bona-fide member to keep up the numbers of the group.

Alice sympathised and pointed out the potential personal outcome of being involved in such a caper. 'Apparently the nerves in his hand are all shot, he could be paralysed for life. We have to be very careful or it will be us that gets put away. You can't do this to people, no matter how bad you feel,' she remarked darkly.

Gregory couldn't help himself and pursued the lighter side. 'He will recover, eventually...until then he is *the* proper one-arm bandit! Do you like that? I've been working on it all day,' he added, laughing like a drain.

But nobody else laughed. A pause indicated the tension developing within the group. To make matters worse, Cuddly Ken spelled out the situation. 'Problem is, we didn't get the thief who's been going around doing our machines. He's the one we really needed to get. Of course, he will be laughing all the way to the bank or wherever it is he puts the money. We have injured the wrong man! OK, he will think twice before doing it again, but just imagine the outcry if a child had put his hand in. A thing like that could kill a child. We can't do any more like this. No, no – we'll have to think again.'

'OK, OK, OK,' came the replies as they hung up.

'Stay on the line, will you, Gregory?' Derek requested, but it was too late: Gregory had also pressed the end-call button.

Derek was not satisfied with the way the conference call had ended; he wanted answers and action but all he got was, 'Let's think again.' He was sitting in his car and looking at his basic but informative accounts sheet. It did not make good reading.

He gripped the steering wheel of his car and fumed. 'If I lose one machine a week, with its cash and stock, I am five hundred quid down the river. That effectively wipes out any profit and, as a result, I am operating at a loss. Well, it can't go on.'

Gregory was also feeling a bit low; he felt as though he had done his best and, in his mind, he'd been successful. 'It's a shame the others don't see it as a success but they're just not on my wavelength,' he thought, as he packed away the components of his latest gadget.

Fortunately, not everyone had abandoned him. He felt the phone vibrating in his jacket pocket. 'Fuck's this?' he grumbled as he retrieved it. He looked at the screen. 'Hello, Derek. I thought you and the others had fallen out with me. I didn't think you would be contacting me again. After all, it got a bit personal at the end.'

'Never mind that, let's meet. Where do you suggest?'

'Come round to my place. I'll have the kettle on.'

Derek had always been a bit wary of Gregory; he was grateful for his help but, like the other members of COG, he had reservations about how far his friend would go in order to achieve an end. He entered the sparsely decorated lounge to find the woodchip and white walls decked with photos of Gregory in military uniform but about five stone lighter.

'Tea or coffee?' Gregory asked, as he came in from the kitchen.

'Coffee is fine. Where were these taken?'

'I did about three years abroad. I'm still twitchy now after another five years. I got out in one piece but loads of my mates didn't. I still see some of them – most have bits missing. I don't know how they cope. I'm in one piece and I'm struggling.'

Derek was beginning to think that his problems were miniscule compared to what Gregory had to put up with. He looked at the other pictures; the soldiers leaning on the military vehicles all seemed to be smiling.

'They seem happy enough,' Derek suggested as Gregory put down the cups.

'Not many of them left. I keep thinking I'll put a line through the ones that didn't make it, but then I don't. It seems wrong.'

They let the coffee cool enough to drink and their minds settled. Derek could see Gregory was still troubled and decided to tread carefully. 'So what did you make of the comments? I suppose they had a point about the chance of kids being injured.'

Gregory looked at him and took a mouthful of coffee. 'I know we didn't get the right man but, trust me, word will have got around that you can't just rob a machine and get away with it. When they hear about what happened and the state that the guy is in now, they'll think twice before going anywhere near another machine.'

'So you think that it's sorted, then?'

'I'm not saying that. What I am saying is that you should be OK in the short term.'

Derek was disappointed with Gregory's assumption that all would be OK. He offered a proposal that would allow him to rest easier, whilst offering Gregory some meaningful purpose. 'How about I accept what you say but in the meantime you come up with a gadget that will deter the thief if I get machines broken into again?'

Gregory nodded and stood up. 'Just hang on. I might have what you are looking for.' He came back carrying the inside of a machine wired onto a board. 'See this? This one is electronically tagged so that if anyone interferes with it an alarm goes off. Do you want to hear it?'

'Er no, that's OK...I'm sure it's deafening.'

'Oh, it is.' Gregory could see that Derek was unimpressed and put the circuit board down on the table.

'I've been thinking,' said Derek, trying not to be too hard on Gregory's efforts. 'The point is – and if I can put it militarily for you – it's not the soldiers we should be going for, it's the bleeding generals. It's Mr Big we should be after, or his property. The thief will just be replaced.'

'I've thought about stuffing one with explosives and then, when the thief tampers with it, it will blow his head off.' Gregory waddled on his seat with excitement.

'Er no,' replied Derek. 'You're not listening. What we need, if my machines get done again, is a device that can be switched on remotely at Mr Big's premises. Something that will wreck his business in one go.' It was his turn to waddle on his seat.

Gregory smiled as he began to understand Derek's line of attack. 'Have you got his name or postcode, 'cos we don't know where he lives?'

Some simple advice

Although Geoff didn't fully inform George about the dye being injected onto pound coins and his frantic escape from the shopping mall, George heard all about it from a friend, a trader whose machines miraculously were never touched.

George was alarmed by the new tactics of the coin-slot operators' group and decided to offset their strategy. Normally he would have had a firm response to their actions but this time he was a bit stumped. He was in the workshop discussing the situation with Geoff, who had been up most of the previous night emptying machines way up the motorway. Geoff was tired, and uncontrollable yawns affected his ability to concentrate.

'Are you listening?' George asked. 'Well, you should. I've heard the operators are getting ruthless – they nearly killed a bloke the other day. From now on, you inspect every machine before you touch it. Come on, wake up, or you'll be in bother.'

Geoff slid off the bench he was sitting on and did his best to wake up; he widened his eyes and rubbed his face with his palms in an effort to inject some attention. 'OK, I'm right now, George. What are we looking for? It's got to be obvious 'cos I've only got seconds at a machine then I'm out of there.'

'It's difficult to say, but you're looking for things out of the ordinary – wires dangling from the back, people standing near the machines who look suspicious. Oh, I don't know, but keep your wits about you from now on. Goodness knows what they did to the insides of the machine the other day but it nearly took that bloke's hand off. Massive burns. Apparently he is gibbering idiot now, can't speak or stop shaking.'

On hearing that, Geoff stood more upright.

'You've got to take this seriously,' George went on. 'It's like it's no-holds barred from now on. And on top of that, I believe they have got an ex-army nutter on board who is willing to put some gadgetry inside the machines that could do real damage. From what I've heard, he thinks he's still doing war games.'

'OK, I'll be careful – even though I don't know what I'm looking for.'

There are no pockets in shrouds

To Angela, the days seemed to have lengthened since she'd lost her job at the school. She was only an assistant there, but her strategy was that as long as she was keen and flexible in her outlook she could fit into any teaching situation and, as a consequence, be a highly regarded member of the staff. What she didn't bank on was the school merging with another one; all of a sudden there were just too many assistants, and last in was first out.

At first she took having extra time on her hands as a positive; it gave her the freedom to do whatever she wanted whilst at the same time she looked for another job. It was only when she started to fill in application forms that she realised just how unskilled she was for anything outside of education. She didn't fancy checkout jobs so she booked into classes to be creative but, after just a few weeks, that fizzled out.

Motivation was the issue; she couldn't get herself going to apply for any old job, so she decided to bide her time till something came along that she felt would suit her better. In the meantime, she was hoping that having a project would occupy her mind and give her inner spirit a kick up the backside. Unfortunately it didn't. Also she became worried that she was losing her vim and vigour; lethargy had crept into her life in the form of daytime TV.

'After switching on the telly, the hours can fly by. Meaningless documentaries initially grab your attention, your brain switches off, and before you know it the day has gone. Well, it has to stop,' she instructed herself. 'A different strategy is required, one that is guaranteed to generate enthusiasm...and in order to support it, I'm going to chuck some money at it.'

But that wasn't going to be straightforward either so, until an answer to the problem materialised, she sat on a stool in the gloomy confines of the old garage looking at the rows and rows of shelves groaning with the weight of cash-filled tea caddies. She was thinking deeply about the money situation. In the past twelve months she and Geoff had gone from arguing about the lack of money and how they were going to survive without her wage, to arguing about what they were going to do with the ten-grand redundancy money – spend it on a new job or a kitchen, or invest it.

'And now we have all this money, he won't let me spend any of it in case we get rumbled, so now we argue about that.'

Her mind whizzed with speculation then, in a symbolic gesture of defiance, she held up two fingers to the shelves. 'Well, guess what? Oh, and by the way, that one is mine,' she said tapping a brightly coloured metal box lid.

A few days later, as a result of the need to be creative and at the same time improve the quality their life, she pushed Geoff out onto the streets with a large shopping list and strict instructions not to return until tea time. He didn't understand but he was too tired to argue; thinking that she was just going to paint a wall, he accepted the orders and left.

As he was pulling away in his car, a large van halted adjacent to their front door. 'Someone must be having work done. Why can't they park outside their own door?' he grumbled miserably.

He had a mixed day. Firstly, he couldn't understand why he had to go to the furthest part of town to buy kitchen utensils when he could have bought them around the corner; secondly, when he'd bought everything on the list and he decided to get some much-needed sleep in a municipal car park, a gardener started up a deafening motorised strimmer. Geoff tried protesting but the man said he was only doing his job.

Not wanting to be beaten, Geoff decided on another tack. If he couldn't get some sleep, a relaxing coffee would pass the time and keep him awake. 'Free papers and soft armchairs… luxury,' he thought.

Unfortunately the coffee didn't work either. A young waitress tapped him on the shoulder and respectfully asked him if he could stop snoring because other customers were complaining.

'Really? OK, sorry, but I don't snore,' he said, trying to reassure the waitress who replied softly, 'But you do.'

So, after a short walk it was time to return home even if he was a bit early. 'How long does it take to paint a wall?' he thought as he walked up the path.

The smell of sawdust and paint greeted him as he opened the door. Not knowing what to expect he walked straight in.

'What do you think?' Ange asked as he entered.

'I think I need to get some kip.'

'No, what do think about the new kitchen? It only took a day.'

He smiled enthusiastically, then wandered around opening cupboards and sliding out drawers. 'Hey, this is alright. I'm impressed. Who did it?'

'That new shop on the supermarket estate.'

'Dare I ask how much?'

'You can ask,' she replied playfully.

'Oh come on, Ange, how much?'

'Seven grand, give or take a few quid. But we can afford it.'

'Seven grand!! Did he take a cheque?'

'Partly. I gave him a cheque for two grand and a caddy for five.'

'You gave him a caddy?'

'Yes, he didn't mind. I had to ask him to lift it down 'cos I couldn't manage it.'

Geoff went over to the new breakfast bar and put his head in his hands. Ange sat next to him and ran her hands over the new worktop. 'Do you like it?'

'I love it… It's just that now everyone will know what we have in the garage. Did you not think about that?'

'He was well impressed with the caddies. He said if you want him to come back, he will put us some proper shelves up.'

'I'll bet he did.'

The candlelit meal served at the breakfast-cum-dining table was very tasty but did little to settle Geoff's nerves. Luckily several glasses of red wine calmed his fears, but they also reduced his ability to walk. Ange assisted her jelly-legged husband upstairs. He was asleep before his head hit the pillow but, within hours, as the alcoholic effect faded, dreams of amputated arms and empty shelves filled his mind.

A few days go by with Spade not reporting in

Spade had settled into his new job. He was walking to the factory for the evening shift and assessing the situation. 'No worries so far. No bosses breathing down my neck, so I might as well carry on working on the production line. I have to build up relationships in order to gain information and so far I've gained nothing other than sleep deprivation.'

He had not gone undercover like this before and found it curious that he had assumed two separate lives. As time went on, he became more relaxed and less inclined to make mistakes, though he was aware he had to keep his story simple and make sure he sang from the same hymn sheet. Unfortunately, the longer the job went on, the more he felt he had to reveal; he started to feel awkward lying to his co-worker Alf, who, until now, had treated him very well. Now and again Spade wondered how Alf would feel when he eventually had to confess that it was a necessary sham in order to solve the mystery of the two corpses.

On his way through to his conveyor, he passed the notice about the five-a-side. 'Digger was right. If I'm going to get to know the others, I need a ploy. The five-a-side should do it.'

He looked across the conveyor belt. 'Alf?' he shouted to his new friend, who was waiting for the whistle to blow that would announce the start of the shift. 'Alf, when is the five-a-side kick-about?'

'Didn't think you were bothered. Last time we spoke, you didn't show any interest.'

'I've slept since then.'

'Saturday morning, ten o'clock on the car park.'

Spade held up his thumb to indicate approval. As the whistle blew, it drowned out his muttering. 'First it was my nights, now it's my weekends as well. Shit.'

Game on

There was no late shift on Friday so Spade should have had a full night's sleep. 'No chance,' he muttered whilst staring at the ceiling. The questions were going round in his head.

'What do I wear? Can't turn up in fancy gear, they'll think I'm a right show-off and I'll become a target. No, got to keep it low key, let them think I don't care. Just jeans and a T-shirt is too scruffy. Old T-shirt, holiday shorts and a pair of worn-out trainers, that should do it. So how do I play it? They look a rough crew. Is it a friendly kick-about or is there more at stake, inter-employee league or something? Oh I don't know, but I can't become the focus. I've got to mix in, otherwise it will all be a waste of time.'

He went downstairs for a cup of tea, hoping that his mind would settle down and he'd be able to grab the remaining hours' sleep.

He arrived early, kitted out, but was surprised to find the car park already marked out with cones for five-a-side. The others, who Spade only knew by sight, were warming up, their deep breaths visible in the crisp, cool air. Luckily their clothing was casual, as expected, and he wondered how they would identify the different teams. Within minutes he found out.

'Here, put this on,' said Alf holding out a yellow armband.

'Ah, the dirty yellows,' Spade replied, as he stretched it over his elbow and up to his T-shirt sleeve. He looked around at his team members and the opposition; nobody was smiling. 'Gosh! They all look so serious about the game. This is not to going to be a friendly,' he thought, exhaling deeply.

The referee, who Spade vaguely recognised, was also casually dressed apart from a black T-shirt to indicate his authority. He stepped onto the centre of the makeshift pitch, bouncing the ball, then he blew the whistle to gain attention and put the ball on the centre spot. 'OK, you know the rules. You have two fifteen-minute halves. Keep it clean, no punching or gouging,' at which point he laughed and blew the whistle again to start the game.

'More like a boxing match,' Spade grumbled as the ball came his way followed by two opposition players.

He was immediately bundled off the ball and dumped down on the tarmac. Despite his protests, the referee said he saw nothing and play continued. Spade picked himself up and watched as the furious play gained in speed, physicality and noise. Players screamed for the ball to be passed to them. Spade decided that possession of the ball had no place here and that survival was the priority, so he immediately forwarded any ball passed to him to another team member.

Before long the game was over; as they walked off, grazes were compared like battle scars but, on the whole, it had been a light-hearted kick-about. By the time they had vacated the playing area, more teams had taken to the pitch and the whistle was blown to announce the start of play.

Watching from the touchline, Spade was amazed at the fouls and dirty tactics that went unnoticed. He hadn't expected an audience and it took him by surprise that a considerable number of girlfriends and family members had turned up to watch. The office staff were also showing support; they didn't have any favourites, they just liked watching men in shorts running around and sweating. After the game they would get in a huddle and award marks out of ten.

Spade wondered about his limited disguise. He hadn't shaved for almost a month and assumed he wouldn't be recognised but Gillian, who was watching the game from the other side of the factory railings, spotted him instantly. She smiled then tentatively waved; he smiled back whilst trying not to raise attention.

Further along the railings the bespectacled secretary from the office, who was still smarting over the treatment she'd received through the office window, recognised Spade and an opportunity to get even.

After all the games had been completed, Spade made a point of locating Alf, who had been a member of an opposing team.

'Cracking game. Did you enjoy it?' said Alf, still gasping and sweating.

'Oh yes,' Spade replied, showing him his scuffed elbows and knees.

'Coming to the pub after? The landlord has put on a breakfast for us, full fry-up with all the trimmings.'

'What, free?'

'Don't worry, he gets his money back from all the beer they sup. First pint doesn't usually touch the sides, then it's a continuous queue at the bar.'

'Wouldn't miss it,' Spade nodded. A feeling of guilt wafted over him; he was sure Alf was innocent regarding the missing persons and he felt awkward stringing him along. He had to keep reminding himself that it was a job, a job he had to do to solve the mystery.

'Digger was spot on and the plan is working, despite having to deceive a nice friendly guy,' he said to himself.

As described, the plates of breakfast were served speedily and consumed without ceremony. The 'plague of locusts' re-enactment made Spade feel queasy. 'Resembles feeding time at a piggery,' he said under his breath as he fiddled with his food. As he poked a sausage around, he felt eyes looking at his plate then at him.

'Are you not going to eat it?' asked his table companion, who had finished his meal ages ago.

'Not that hungry,' Spade replied.

Without hesitation, the man swapped plates and set about the remains of Spade's meal as though he hadn't eaten for a week. Spade rose from his seat and left him to it. It was then he noticed a hive of activity at the end of the bar; individuals were pointing down a list until they found their name, then either smiling or frowning. 'Better go over,' he thought.

He pondered the names but couldn't recognise his own. Luckily his friend Alf was close by. 'Harry Jones, you are on our side,' Alf shouted.

'So I am,' Spade shouted back. He rubbed his forehead and widened his eyes. 'Wake up, boy, or you will fuck this up,' he muttered to himself.

He hadn't realised but five-a-side was only the start of the activities; darts were next and dominoes later, all accompanied by several pints of foaming brew. The event grew in fervour and Spade became aware of the heady haze and lack of control created by free-flowing beer.

'Not good, not good, got to reel it in a bit,' he thought.

He withdrew from the arena of play and staggered his way to the gents. After standing at the urinal, he faced the mirror over the sink. Struggling with his mental clarity, he decided on a cold wash and some fresh air. He splashed his face several time to revive his senses then, after drying it on a paper towel, stepped through the back door of the pub and entered the smoking area

'This is worse,' he muttered. On the cobbled street behind the pub the air was less contaminated. The effect of breathing in cold air had a partially sobering effect, which Spade was grateful for, but he still felt wobbly and not entirely alert.

He walked up and down the street, breathing heavily in an effort to expel the alcoholic effects. As he turned to do another lap, a question was posed to him from the confines of the back door of the pub. 'Enjoy the game?'

It was the referee, who Spade now recognised as the workforce organiser in the factory. He turned to face him; luckily he was feeling more like his quick-thinking self. 'Survived. No damage to speak of, despite your lack of intervention,' he said with a titter in his voice that hid the way he really felt.

'Can't keep stopping the game. There's only thirty minutes – there'd be no play at all if I kept blowing the whistle. Anyway, you managed to keep out of trouble. Are you sure you enjoyed it?'

'It's not the winning, it's the taking part,' Spade replied frankly. 'No point breaking bones on Saturday or there'll be no work on Monday.'

'Talking of work, I believe you've been asking about the man you replaced,' the referee said.

'Just out of common curiosity,' Spade said, trying to show only a passing interest.

The ref stood forward a pace and his face changed from pacifist to aggressor. 'Well you know what happened to the cat!'

Spade did not reply; he stared back at the man who eventually turned and went back into the pub. 'It appears the plan *is* working,' he thought with a smirk. 'In fact, I seem to have touched a very sensitive nerve. Going to have to move things along, though. I can't work here forever, no way.'

He wandered back into the pub and observed the players getting more and more stupefied. Beer was getting spilt, the noise level was increasing to deafening pitch and tempers were getting frayed. 'Crikey, this is going to kick off any minute now,' he mumbled from a safe distance.

It was only a game of dominoes but, after accusations of swan necking (spying your opponent's dominoes), a bit of shoving and pushing broke out. Spade wasn't the only one to predict a drunken riot; so did the landlord, who marched in ringing a hand-bell. 'That's it, playtime is over. I hope you all enjoyed yourself but I've got normal customers coming in shortly, so you can all go back to bed. I'll tidy up after you – don't worry about the spilt beer and broken glass. We'll sort it after you leave – which is right now.'

At that moment the bar staff waded in to clear the area, despite the resentment from the players. The group of well-drunk young men found themselves out on the pavement; remarkably, it was still only ten to twelve on a Saturday morning. Discussion ensued about the next pub they should invade but most, including Alf and Spade, decided that enough was enough.

'That's me done,' Spade said to Alf, who had succumbed to sitting on an empty beer barrel, conveniently stacked and waiting to be replaced. Spade walked away and left him stewing in his own alcohol. 'See you Monday,' he shouted, but Alf had nodded off.

After a brisk walk home, Spade reflected on the day. 'It was enjoyable, it was scary at times but, most importantly, I got a result without even trying.'
He forwarded the information to Digger via a text.
'Good man,' Digger replied. 'You can go to bed now.'
And Spade did.

Question time

Sunday, the day of rest and recuperation. Spade lifted his throbbing head off the pillow and considered his condition. 'OK, my head aches like crazy, I could easily throw up, I don't seem to be able to lift my arms... My knees and elbows have stopped bleeding and my back aches where I think I was kicked. All in all, a good day out, so pills, plasters, strong coffee and a long bath.'

It was while he was soaking in the bath that his phone pinged. He reached with dripping hands and retrieved it from the floor. After drying his hands, he swiped across the screen and saw who had called.

'Digger! What the—? I've only just got up, and it's Sunday.'

He went to messages; it was simple: '*What's next?*'

'I could tell you what's next, but I don't want us to fall out,' Spade snapped. He switched off the phone and slid down into the warm, soapy water.

The following day, partially refreshed and still sore, he reported for the evening shift. He sensed an atmosphere; Alf was not exactly ignoring him but he wasn't engaging in conversation either. Spade ignored his one-word answers and thought it must be a mood he was in.

'Did you enjoy Saturday?' Spade asked him.

'Yeah, fine,' Alf replied

'I'm still sore, are you?'

'I'm OK.'

The stilted conversation continued for a while then petered out; eventually relief came in the form of the tea break. The shrill whistle blew to indicate a rest period. People sighed and their bodies flopped with relief; even the machine released tension as it squeaked to a halt. The workers sauntered outside, stretching and yawning. It was cold – four in the morning and the sun had not risen yet – and until they walked under the car-park lighting, they were not visible.

'It's like being in a spooky movie where the dead crawl out of their graves and terrorise the inhabitants,' Spade said to Alf through the side of his mouth. 'Do you like working here? Is this what you dreamed of when you were at school?'

'You ask too many questions!' Alf responded with a trace of fear in his voice.

'Well, do you?'

'Now look, I don't know what you are up to but get off my back... The others are watching.'

They were indeed. Out of the corner of his eye, Spade could see unfriendly faces staring his way. 'Alf, this is not a nice place to work. Can we meet? A pint, maybe, where we won't be disturbed.'

'Who are you? What do you want?'

Alf declined to turn up for a pint and didn't show for the next shift.

Customer care

Ange was happy with the way the kitchen had worked out. 'In fact, it could not have been simpler,' she thought, as she retrieved the still-hot breakfast dishes from the dishwasher and placed them in their new cupboards.

'Never had a dishwasher before, seemed lazy. But hey, this is the cheap end of the market when it comes to gadgetry. We could have had boiling water coming out of the tap, an American-style fridge-freezer, a central-aisle worktop and a double oven. But, as the man said, "bit limited with space, madam".'

The ease with which she'd organised the designer to achieve exactly what she wanted had renewed her confidence in herself. When she'd been made redundant it was a very low point; she'd thought about going to see a stress counsellor but had decided to work her way through it. 'Seems to have worked,' she thought.

She heard a clatter from behind the front door; realising the postman had just called, she walked down the hallway to pick up the morning mail. Immediately she made out a dark silhouette through the frosted glass of the front door. She paused and watched, as did the silhouette.

Looking through the open door to the front room and through the front window, she saw the postman striding purposefully up the street. Almost as soon as he'd disappeared from view, there was a knock at the door. Ange waited and the knock came again. She exhaled, then marched to the door and opened it sharply.

In a loud voice she enquired, 'Yes? What can I do for you?' Recognising the man at the door to be the kitchen fitter, she tempered her voice. 'Yes?' she asked again.

'I was in the area and thought I'd call round to make sure all is OK. Can I come in?'

'What for?'

'Oh, it's best if I just check to make sure there are no leaks.'

'There are no leaks.'

'Ah, not to the naked eye... And, while I'm here, it's best if I check to make sure the fridge is getting down to the right temperature.'

'I'm going out in a few minutes. You won't be long, will you?'

'I'll be gone before you know it.'

Ange walked behind him as they went down the hall. 'No tools? Kitchen fitters are usually loaded with tools.'

He ignored her comment and continued towards the kitchen. He touched the worktops and turned the hob extractor on then off. 'Everything OK?' he queried.

'It's fine. Now, if you don't mind, I have to go out.'

'Actually, when we did the sums it turns out we didn't charge you enough.'

They glared at one another and Ange could feel her face reddening. 'Didn't you? Well, I'm sorry, but a deal is a deal. If you would like to go over the paperwork again, I think you'll find that I've paid you everything that you are due. So come on, out – before I get angry!'

The man stood his ground and leaned back casually against the worktop edge. 'You can afford it.'

Ange squinted; she knew where he was going with this but decided to play ignorant. 'You have got all I am prepared to pay. My husband Geoff thinks I've paid over the odds as it is. He certainly won't want to pay any more, so I think you better pack your bags.'

'Now look, lady—'

'Don't you fucking lady me.'

There was a momentary stand-off as each searched for the next ploy. The man played his ace. 'I don't know what you and your husband are up to, but you can bet your boots it's fishy. I bet the police would like to find out just how you managed to stash thousands and thousands of pound coins.'

'None of your business what we are up to. But beware of what you wish for, 'cos it could come back and bite you on your arse.' Ange turned away from the man to let him digest her comments. In front of her was the rack containing the cooking implements.

Suddenly the man, seemingly in desperation, leapt at her and grabbed her by the throat. 'I'm going to take some of those coins, whether you like it or not,' he shouted hysterically.

'OK, OK,' she said, choking. 'But we've moved them. The caddies are now on a shelf under the worktop.'

He paused. Thinking she had succumbed to his demands, he released his grip and looked down to where he thought the caddies were stored. Inside Ange, rage took over. She looked at the rack and, in a flash and without thinking twice, she grabbed a meat tenderiser. She swung it in a wide arc, hitting the fitter on the back of the head, clean and hard. He dropped like a stone with just one twitch and a gasping exhalation.

'Oh fuck, this morning is not going to plan,' Ange thought.

She stared at the lifeless body for ages in disbelief and sadness that it should have turned out like this. 'But you started it,' she mumbled to the corpse.

There was surprisingly little to clean up but, just in case, she went into her newly stocked broom cupboard and donned rubber gloves and an unused floral apron. Then she set about the spilt but minimal bodily fluids with paper towels from the new, wall-mounted dispenser.

'Irony, I like a bit of irony. You installed all of this and the first time I get to use it is when I'm cleaning up your mess.'

She chuckled as she put the hammer in the dishwasher and set the dial to deep clean. She threw the clothes and the apron into the new washing machine and set it to run at maximum temperature. With all the machines buzzing away, she went upstairs for a shower. 'Shame you didn't revamp the bathroom, but maybe the next fitter won't be as greedy,' she shouted to the corpse.

After a shower and a coffee, she felt amazingly relaxed – despite having a dead body in the kitchen. Sitting close to the window so she could catch Geoff before he entered the house, she wondered how she was going to break the news. Fortunately she did not have long to wait.

She let him park the car then opened the door for him. Right away he suspected something. 'Oh, what's up?'

'Don't go in yet.'

'Why?'

'You were right about the man and the shelves. But don't worry, I've taken care of it.'

'You've taken care of it… How?'

They walked in silence into the kitchen and stared at the now-covered corpse.

'Please explain,' he moaned.

'Firstly, he said was coming to check the kitchen, which was a lie. Then he said he wanted more money so I told him to push off. He got angry. He said he would phone the police and tell them we were up to no good and that we had a garage full of money. I told him again to push off – and it was then that he tried to strangle me. So I said I would give him some more money if he let go of my throat. When he wasn't looking, I hit him with the mallet. That's it in a nutshell. But nobody knows he's here – it's his day off. His van is at the depot.'

'Mallet … what mallet?'

They looked across at the rack containing cooking implements; one hook was empty.

'It's part of the new kitchen utensils, a steel mallet for tenderising steak. It's a big heavy thing, heavier than I thought. He just went down. No struggle, no nothing, just dead.'

'You know we will never be able to use it again? I mean, it'll all come back every time you use it,' said Geoff, thinking ahead.

'I washed it, hottest setting. Should get rid of any evidence. I did the same with all my clothes. This new kitchen has really come in handy.'

A flicker of a smile drifted across Geoff's face. 'Lucky for us he showed you how to operate the machines then.'

There was momentary silence as they both worked out a plan.

'If we tell the police it could be manslaughter or murder, depending on whether they believe you,' Geoff said. 'Plus the shit would hit the fan about the money.'

'Nobody knows he called here. He was hiding in the bushes till the postman left. It's his day off and his van is in the works compound,' she reassured him.

'You better go and put your old clothes on. Looks like I'm going to get my new garage sooner than I thought.' Geoff rummaged in his pocket for his phone. 'Hello? Yes, it's me, Geoff. That concrete base for the new garage we talked about, I'll be ready tomorrow if you want to send your lorry round. That's right, about two cubic meters should do it. Nine tomorrow is fine. See you then.'

He looked at Ange; he was waiting for a stream of questions but all she said was, 'So?'

'So we shift everything out of the garage, strip him of any ID, wallets, cash, phone, keys and trash them. We'll put them on the fire and bury the remains with him. We'll dig a big deep hole in the garage, put him in it, level it off, tamp it down hard and the concrete man arrives at nine tomorrow. Simple.'

'Have you done this before?'

The show must go on

Spade turned up for the night shift and clocked on. Usually this activity was an occasion for light-hearted banter and a bit of pushing and shoving as the workers fought to avoid clocking-in late. He felt a chill when he saw that he was alone; he checked the time on the clock to see if he was either early or late, but he was bang on.

He walked through the floppy plastic screen that separated the entrance from the production line to find all the other workers standing at their work stations and staring at him. As he approached his point on the conveyor, he was surprised to find that he had a new partner.

He waved and attempted chit-chat but there was no reply. 'Suit yourself, but it's a long shift,' he shouted, in an attempt to show that he was going to carry on as normal despite their refusal to communicate.

Out of the corner of his eye, he noticed the white flash of a freshly laundered smock. He turned and was confronted by the supervisor holding up his clipboard. He ran his pen down the list of names. 'Ah … Harry Jones, if that is your name. Didn't expect to see you here today,' he said with a certain menace as he put a tick against Spade's pseudonym.

'Oh, why?' Spade asked.

'No reason, I just thought that you didn't particularly enjoy our little outing the other day. You seemed a bit on the periphery, kind of outside looking in.' He dropped the clipboard by his side and moved closer. 'There are people here who think that you are not who you say you are. You've been poking your nose in where you shouldn't. Be warned,' he said, pointing towards his nose. 'Keep it out, or you might not make it to the end of the shift.'

'Seen anything of Alf?' Spade asked flippantly.

'Be warned,' the supervisor threatened again.

Spade continued to man the production line but, as the shift wore on, it became apparent that moves were afoot to silence him, either in the short term or perhaps for longer, neither of which appealed. When the whistle blew, he shuffled outside with the others then slipped to one side into an unlit doorway. Unfortunately, as soon as he switched on his phone it illuminated his position.

'Yes, I know it's four thirty but I'm beginning to feel that my cover is blown. From a point of personal safety, I should be on my way,' he advised Digger, who was half asleep.

'Look, don't mess about, just get yourself out. We can discuss it all tomorrow.'

At that point, an unrecognised voice took over the conversation. 'Who am I speaking to?' Digger asked.

'Never mind that, who are you?' the voice demanded.

Spade was surrounded and his phone was crushed under the supervisor's foot,.

'Phoning your dad, were you? OK, put him in the little store. Get back to your conveyors and we'll sort him out later.'

Spade was frog-marched back into the factory, down a gloomy alleyway and bundled into a dimly lit store room. He heard the door slam and the metallic click of the lock. He picked himself up and rubbed his eyes, then realised that he was in semi-darkness. As he became accustomed to the limited light, he could make out shelving containing chemicals, cleaning equipment and some heavy tools.

'A fine how-do-you-do. Never mind, a squad of heavily armed riot police will be surrounding the building as I speak. But just in case … I should find a way out of this place.'

The crumbly and elderly nature of the factory provided chinks of light around the door frame and knot holes in the door; these gave Spade a limited but useful vision of the outside. To one side, if he strained, he could make out the familiar framework of the conveyor. The noise was quite loud so he surmised that he was at the top end of the factory, furthest from the exit doors.

As he peered through the spy hole, a person walked past then, moments later, back again. 'Ah, a sentry,' Spade thought. 'Gosh, I must be important.'

His eyesight was improving and he could now read the numerals on his watch. 'Bloody hell, ages to go yet and sadly I can't hear any sirens or the crashing of hobnailed boots. Looks like it's up to me.'

He watched as the sentry walked back and forth. The lock was on the outside of the door but the metal handle reached through both sides. 'All that theory about lock-picking – what a waste. I can't even reach the bloody lock but, with a bit of luck, they won't have chosen the sharpest knife in the drawer to march up and down. So, there's about an hour to go. I need to be out of here well before the end of the shift. It'll still be pandemonium out there so I should get some cover.'

An old vacuum cleaner abandoned in the corner gave him an idea.

'Help, help, I think you've broken my arm. I feel sick!' he shouted through the small hole in the door. He watched for the man to pass the door then immediately yelled for help again. 'If I die of shock from my injuries it will be your fault. You'll be convicted of manslaughter and sent down for a long, long time, mixing with other murderers who will beat you senseless if you don't bow to their needs. You don't want that, do you? Well, I don't think I can last much longer.'

'What's wrong?' the sentry whispered to the door.

'I feel sick and faint and about to pass out. You broke my arm and it will be your fault if you don't do something. Hurry!' he urged.

Spade heard the key enter the lock. 'Patience,' he muttered.

He waited until the key had turned then watched for movement of the handle. The moment it jiggled, he switched on the electrical power at the socket on the wall. He had stripped the cable from the vacuum and connected it to the handle.

Spade heard the guttural cry of someone in agony; he let the screams continue for a while then switched it off. 'Should be cooked by now,' he mused as he opened the door.

The sentry, now in the foetal position, was holding his shaking hand. As he saw Spade, he realised that he had been duped and attempted to grab Spade's leg.

'I haven't time for this,' Spade said, hitting the man on his good hand with a spanner. 'Now look, stay down or you'll get another.'

The sentry cowered and waved that he understood.

'OK, this is not going to be easy but the alternatives have not presented themselves yet,' Spade said.

He approached the end of the conveyor on his hands and knees. He kept low; production was slowing but still continuing, and he could see that the conveyor finished just short of the warehouse exit. He decided that this was his only opportunity to escape.

Ducking under the still-speeding conveyor belt was scary and he gritted his teeth as he entered into the hollow tunnel beneath. He was in close proximity to the flapping belt, the chains and electric motors that drove it. Further up, he could almost touch the legs and feet of the attendant worker. Even though there was some head room, he slithered along on his stomach.

'Keep low or there will be another head to investigate,' Spade kept telling himself as he climbed through gaps he never thought he would fit through. At two-metre intervals brackets spanned across the support legs; this meant he had to slide over them and get even closer to the rattling belt.

Halfway along, he heard the electric motors slow down, indicating that the end of the shift was near. He shook his head in despair and scrambled faster but this put him at risk of getting entangled in the belt. It seemed as though the faster he scrambled, the louder the machine clattered and the greater was the chance he would get trapped in it.

'No mistakes now. I can't get caught under here.'

His knees and hands were bleeding from clambering over rough concrete and sharp-edged steel. 'Keep going,' he kept repeating to spur himself on.

As he crawled along, he felt it strange that the legs of the workers were so close but they had no inkling that he was there. He reached the end of the machine and heard the whistle blow for the end of the shift. The noise receded and the conveyor belt finally stopped. Spade held his breath as the workers stepped down from the platform alongside the conveyor. They headed towards the store whilst he scrambled out and ran in the opposite direction through the warehouse and out into the open. He kept on running until he reached the main street of the village.

He looked down at his hands and knees. He knew where the taxi rank was situated and set off. 'Oh, and what happened to the bleeding cavalry then?' he grumbled, as he brushed the muck and dust off his pants with his scuffed hands.

How was I to know?

Digger sat in his office. He knew that Spade had blown his cover but he did not know how serious it was. He was also unaware that Spade's phone had been trashed by the supervisor. 'Either way, he wouldn't appreciate me ringing him this early in the morning after being up all night.'

He was right. After a hot shower that highlighted all the areas where he'd been injured, Spade decided on a cup of tea and a couple of hours' kip. After lunch he intended to go into work but found that, as he made his way downstairs, he could hardly walk. He ached all over and his elbows and knees smarted so much that he decided against it. He rang in instead.

'Are you OK?' Digger enquired when he recognised Spade's voice.

'I've been better. It's a long story but I only just escaped this morning. Anyway, it's all gone pear-shaped at the factory. Good timing, I think – I don't think I could get any closer and it was all getting a bit nasty. That gangmaster chap is a bit vicious and the one guy I thought I could speak to, Alf, has gone missing. I'm a bit worried about him.'

There was a moment of silence as Spade reflected on his experience. 'I thought I was a goner this morning, my very existence on the line. I was convinced that you'd have twigged that something was up and that you would have sent the cavalry to get me. What happened?'

'Firstly, your phone just went dead. How was I to know that the reason it went dead was because it had been trodden on? I'm not a mind reader and, in any case, I can't get a force of men together at this time in the morning. They're all in bed.'

'So let me get this straight. Before the next time I get in bother I have to check the sleep patterns of the heavy mob. Is that right?' Spade remarked with an element of displeasure.

'Well, you seem OK. Proper night's sleep and you'll be right as rain.'

'I'll send you the hospital bill... So what are we going to do about Alf? I've an awful feeling that he's been more than just warned off.'

'Whilst you recover, I'll ring around and put the word out.'

'Oh, and I need a new phone.'

To change the mood, Digger made light of his request. 'Have you seen the amount of paperwork required to get a replacement? It's in triplicate and you have to get witness statements with dates and times. Besides, you should claim against the factory.'

'Really?' Spade replied, not quite getting the joke.

Sensing Spade's frame of mind, Digger offered a plan. 'OK, so after you've recuperated, we should go and see Granville, the owner of the mill. He's messed us about long enough. What do you say?'

'That's fine,' Spade groaned.

An announcement

Ange was amazed how quickly the new garage was erected; it was as though it was pre-planned and all that was needed was Geoff to say when. It had narked her that it must have been in the back of Geoff's mind all along but, despite her feelings on the subject, it still went ahead.

'Concrete's hardly set,' she said to Geoff, as she tapped it with her foot to test its solidity. 'It doesn't bother you what's underneath, then? I mean, do you not get a shudder every time you stand here? Cos I do...I can't switch off to it like you can. I still see him slumped in the kitchen. I didn't mean to kill him, it were just rage, and the hammer was there in front of me. If it had been a gun, I would have shot him. I wish it hadn't happened and well... I'm sorry Geoff, but I'm not sure I can live here any more.'

Geoff finished admiring the gleaming new concrete interior of the garage; he was just about to measure up for shelving when he comprehended her last statement. 'We have a new kitchen, which you went ahead and ordered without speaking to me. We now have a new garage as a result of your uncontrollable temper. Money is coming in fast and we now have somewhere proper to store it – and now you say you can't live here any more! Well remember, you killed him!'

He threw the tape-measure down onto the floor and walked out. 'I'm off to the pub,' he shouted as he left.

Ange stood in shocked silence. She had expected a bit more understanding and her thoughts were in turmoil. 'It was a major incident. I'd give anything to turn the clock back but I can't. And it happened right here. We buried him right here! Jesus, I'm standing right over it and it will always be there, and all he's bothered about is his bleeding shelves! Well, thanks for nothing.'

Back to basics

Derek's work pattern had changed. Originally it was just a case of putting the machines on the wall or on the stand, filling them with goods, giving it a few days then emptying the cash box and filling the machines with goods again. However, the spate of break-ins now meant that, unless a machine was in a secure location, it was taken home and stored. Trashed machines were taken out of service because they were too expensive to repair. All in all, the number of machines that generated income was decreasing and, as a consequence, so were his earnings.

'A downward spiral that has to be stopped!' he bellowed, whilst hitting the steering wheel with his hand.

It had been a while since he'd heard from Gregory so, on his way home from work, he decided to call in. On opening the door, Gregory welcomed him – a bit over the top, Derek thought.

'Come on in, good to see you,' Gregory said.

They walked into the lounge; it resembled a student's flat – a student that had stopped caring.

'If I'd known you were coming I'd have tidied up,' Gregory said, laughing as he gathered the empty beer cans from the floor.

'Hard at it, I see,' muttered Derek, looking at the blaring TV.

'Let me turn this off. It's just for background noise. Sometimes you catch a good programme but it's rare these days – just repeats.'

As Gregory was filling the kettle, Derek posed the question. 'Let's cut to the quick. Is there any progress with your latest solution to my problem?'

'Funny you should mention that,' Gregory replied cautiously.

'Come on then, out with it.'

'Well, er, I wasn't sure if you were up for it. Most of the others seemed to be dead against it, and I thought maybe you'd been influenced by them into buying the more expensive machines.'

'I've no money, simple as that. And I'm still getting machines turned over. Anyway, as I recall we were talking about sorting it by putting Mr Big's business out of action, his workshop or office or whatever. Problem is, we don't know where it is.'

'I've been thinking about that. We need to follow the thief's trail back to Mr Big. It's going to be awkward because we have to get the thief to read a letter.'

'Read a letter?'

'Yeah, read a letter that we are going to stick on one of your machines.'

'And what will this letter say?'

'The envelope will be addressed to Mr Repair Man and inside will be a letter that says something like: "I am broken but full of money. If you repair me you can keep it".'

'Really? And how is he going to fall for that?'

'Because we are going to press his greedy button.'

'OK. Hardly any cost involved, so I'll go with that. I suppose everybody has a greedy button. Any biscuits to go with this tea?'

Should be easy?

During the absence of his heroic colleague, Inspector Digger applied himself to what he initially considered was a menial task, that of locating Alf's whereabouts.

'So where do we start?' he muttered to the computer screen. 'Firstly, I don't know his surname and Alf, if that is his first name, could be Alfred, which seems a bit like an old name. Or he could be European, hence Alfredo. I don't know his address, his age, or details of any facial features such as a beard or moustache or colour of his hair, or for that matter, the colour of his skin. We are not even certain that he has come to any harm but if we could rule that out, we might get somewhere.'

Freshly armed with a list of hospitals and medical centres in the area, Digger set about phrasing the questions so that he did not appear amateurish. To get the feel of how it would sound, he spoke out loud as he wrote. '*Do you have an admission that looks like he has been beaten up?* Not bad. How about: *Has anyone come to the A&E that looks like he has fallen downstairs? Or fallen off a bicycle? Or all of them.* That's it … all of them. Oh: *And he's probably called Alf.*'

After speaking to several admissions' secretaries, he felt like he had struck lucky.

'Yes,' one secretary told him. 'We have a young man, a bit traumatised, bruises to his body and cuts to his face. Won't tell us how he came by such injuries, been in twenty-four hours. We are about to discharge him.'

'No, no, don't do that, not until I've seen him, I'm on my way.'

***

Alf opened his sore eyes. He blinked and began to focus; as his eyes cleared, he noticed a dark shadow beside his bed. It was a man wearing a trenchcoat.

'In your own words, when you're ready,' said Digger, wetting the sharp end of his pencil with his tongue.

'What?' said Alf.

'Don't give me that. I know you've had a hard time. This is your opportunity to get it all off your chest. So start where you want and I will fill in the gaps.'

'They said that if I opened my mouth they would do me in proper.'

'Now look. If we, you and I, do this right, they will go to prison and you will be free to go and get another job. Is that OK?'

'Really? They said if we grassed we would all go to prison.'

Digger sighed audibly. 'So, have you done anything wrong?'

'No.'

'Well, there you are then. Has anyone else done anything wrong?'

Alf hesitated then slowly nodded.

Digger moved closer then turned his ear to Alf. 'Go on then.'

'It were really horrible,' Alf blubbered then started to sob.

A nurse who was passing interrupted the interview. 'What have you done to upset him like this? First he gets beaten up, then you turn up and start interrogating him. How much more does he have to put up with?' She mopped Alf's tears with a tissue then shooed Digger away. 'You'll be alright, the nasty man has gone now,' she soothed.

Alf nodded his head in appreciation and then sniffed noisily. The nurse looked at him with disgust and handed him the tissue before leaving. 'Keep it,' she added, as she closed the door behind her.

The emotional sobbing was quickly dropped as Alf slid from under the covers. He put on his jeans, T-shirt and trainers, went to the door and gently pressed down on the handle. As he eased open the door, he heard a familiar voice. 'Going somewhere?'

'She said you'd gone. I was coming to find you.'

'A likely story… Now, is it here or down at the station?'

Alf sat on the edge of the bed and recounted all he knew about what had happened a few weeks earlier. 'It were really horrible.'

'Yes, yes, I've got that,' said Digger impatiently..

'Well, it were. The shop steward turned up. We hadn't seen him for ages and he seemed really angry and put out. We thought he'd had an argument with the boss, then he went round the factory with a clipboard making a note of all the safety problems. At break time, he called a meeting and rattled off all of the issues such as unguarded machines, fumes and acid spills. He said that the place was too dangerous to work in and after the break he was going to switch off the machines and bring in the local inspector, who would more than likely close down the factory.'

Digger was writing furiously and at the same time getting excited. He could sense a climax. 'Go on,' he urged.

'Well, it was as he said. We all went back in then he called another meeting around the main switch box, which was above the soda process holding tank. We were down on the factory floor. He said he was sorry but that was how it was, and he was going to turn off the power to the machines. Well, as he went towards the main switch, this other bloke – we don't know who he was – climbed up and jumped him and tried to stop him. It was like the Wild West. They both started shouting and screaming and that's the last we saw of them.'

Digger stopped making notes and looked at him. 'What do you mean, that's the last you saw of them?'

'We were stood below and they were fighting above us on the staging around the tank, then they disappeared and it all went quiet. We never saw them again. It were really horrible.'

'So you said.'

'We were all sent home and told to come in for the next shift but warned not to say anything or there would be dire consequences. When we came in the following day, it was like nothing had happened. It felt weird.'

'So who cleaned up?'

'I don't know. It weren't me.'

***

In the office the following day, Digger related the details to Spade

'Gives a new meaning to body soap,' Spade laughed.

'You've not lost your sick sense of humour, then?'

'It's part of my DNA.'

They both laughed as they shuffled papers into envelopes and then looked at the evidence board. The head, still hidden from view in its envelope, reminded them that it was not over yet.

'So what is it? An unfortunate accident? Can't be murder, can it?' Spade asked.

'No, but it is double corporate manslaughter. It can't be right having an open-top tank full of caustic soda. And at this moment we should not lose the impetus.'

They headed towards the factory owner's home.

'Bloody hell look at this,' Spade exclaimed, as they drove through automatic electronically opening gates. 'All this from making soap?'

'Get a life, boy,' Digger threw in, just to show he hadn't lost it.

Spade laughed but could not control his interest in architecture or his deep-seated, bottle-green envy. As they approached the house, his eyes were everywhere, particularly on the many outbuildings and well-cared-for gardens.

'Will you look at this? There must be an army of people looking after this lot.'

'Hey, don't get distracted. We're here to arrest him,' Digger warned him.

They parked up and the crunch of gravel under the tyres alerted the staff to their arrival. As they approached the manor entrance, they paused at a short flight of stone steps leading up to a large door. They looked up to see a well-dressed young man staring down at them. He greeted them with a cheery, 'Can I help you?'

'Let me get up these first and I'll tell you,' Digger replied officiously. 'I am Inspector Digger and this is my colleague Sergeant Spade. We are here to arrest ... sorry, speak to Mr Granville.'

The man smirked then replied, 'I'll see if he's in.'

At that point, Spade asserted his authority. 'You know whether he is in or not, and I assume that is his car over there, so don't mess us about. Just show us where he is or we'll arrest you for hindering an officer in the pursuance of his duty. Understand?'

'Er, yes, OK,' replied the young man, shaken at the prospect of arrest.

'Well done, Spade,' Digger complimented then joined in. 'Come on then, chop chop. Show us where Granville is.'

Now red-faced and welling up, the young man pointed out the route. 'This way.'

They followed him through a series of rooms and corridors, all decorated with expensive-looking furnishings, porcelain and paintings. Finally they reached a dark-oak doorway and the man tentatively knocked on the door.

'I said I was not to be disturbed!' barked a voice.

The young man shrugged and stared at them.

Spade smiled and ushered him to one side. 'Police,' he shouted.

'What the—!'

The door creaked open and both officers smiled. 'You can go now,' Spade said, turning towards the assistant.

They followed Granville into his office and Digger's nose twitched.

'I know what this is about and I can explain,' Granville said.

'Really? So you can explain the two deaths that happened on your premises, the deliberate hiding of the bodies, the hiring of numerous workers whose identities you haven't a clue about or where they have come from, plus sanctioning the beating of an employee until he is hospitalised to maintain his silence. Not to mention the deliberate contravention of the Health and Safety at Work Act. You are in deep, deep trouble. But no problem, you can explain it all – can't you?'

The man sat slumped at his desk. They could see that he was weighing up his options.

'Well?' said Spade.

'Look, we've been going through a bad time. There's problems with the unions and we just can't compete financially with the stuff that's coming in from abroad. As regards the bodies, it was a mistake. I told them to dump the contents of the tank in the sluice outside, you know, the one that leads to the river. Everything should have gone out to sea and nobody would have been any the wiser. But no, the stupid bastards dumped the stuff in the canal. I know it was wrong, but at the time it seemed the only thing to do. I was just trying to protect them and the factory. It's just one big mistake after another – and besides, I can't be responsible for what goes on when I'm not there, can I?'

'So there are body parts in the soap you have sent out. Very nice.'

'It's only soap! You're not going to eat it.'

There was a momentary pause as Digger looked at his notes. 'The manager, what have you done to the manager?'

'Oh him, he's in India sorting out the new factory. Been there a while now. He didn't want to go but he could see the writing on the wall. He knew we weren't competing.'

Digger nodded towards Spade and put a tick against 'the manager'.

'And the other guy who ended up in the tank?'

'I'm not sure. I think he was just a worker,' Granville said.

'Doesn't know… and probably doesn't care,' Digger added to his notes. He smiled and moved closer to the desk, sniffing like a bloodhound. 'So you're never there. You don't see what goes on in your own rotten stinking factory?'

'I've no need to be there,' Granville said, shaking his head.

'Not had a shower today, have you?' suggested Digger, smirking.

Both Spade and Granville looked puzzled.

'The mix – old oil, acid, strong body odour and hot rubber. I'll never forget it. He's lying through his back teeth – he's there every night. He's the man in the rubber suit. Cuff him!'

'Bingo!' shouted Spade, as he moved forward to clip on the handcuffs.

However Granville had other ideas. Standing up behind the desk, he pushed back the chair with his legs and grabbed his long, knife-shaped letter opener.

'Don't be stupid,' grunted Digger, as the man held the knife at arm's length and made thrusting gestures towards them.

'Get over there and turn around,' Granville growled.

'OK, OK,' they said in unison, turning their backs on him as they shuffled towards the door.

'It doesn't have to end like this. If you get a good lawyer, you could get a reduced sentence, from twenty-five down to fifteen years,' Spade pointed out with a snigger.

They waited a while for a response, but none came. All of a sudden it was so quiet they could hear the birds singing outside. They turned around but Granville had disappeared.

Spade pointed to a bookcase that was now slightly ajar. 'Oh good – a sodding priest's hole. When was the last time a person avoided capture by using a priest's hole?'

'Probably three hundred years ago during the English Civil War, but don't worry he'll not get far,' said Digger, jangling a set of keys. 'Because he who holds the keys controls the car. It's an old Indian proverb,' he added, grinning from ear to ear.

'Is it?'

'No, I just made it up.'

'These escape routes usually lead to just outside the boundary wall,' Spade said looking at his watch. 'So he should be heading to his car right now.'

They wandered back through the house towards front door, admiring the décor and commenting on the changes of style the house must have gone through since the time it was built. Outside, Granville sat behind the wheel of his stationary car, staring ahead through the windscreen, distraught.

'Looking for these?' Digger said, baiting the man as he dangled the keys. 'As I said before, Spade, cuff him – but this time to the steering wheel. And we'll let the heavy mob deal with him.' Digger leaned down to the driver's side window. 'Oh … that list of charges we gave you earlier? Add to it threatening police officers with a dangerous weapon.'

'Lovely garden. I believe a south-facing wall is especially beneficial for growing soft fruit,' Spade informed him as they walked away.

An exit strategy

Gregory was beginning to think he had been ignored. It was a few days since Derek's visit and at that time he'd been led to believe that a meeting was imminent. Eventually, when he did get the call, it was not what he expected. 'You can't all come around here … it's a mess,' he said to Derek, who insisted that they would hold a meeting in Gregory's front room.

'You have an hour to tidy up. There will only be four of us in total. Seemed daft to have a formal meeting, so we'll meet at your place.'

After a quick wash and brush up, Gregory vacuumed the downstairs rooms whilst throwing old newspapers and beer cans into a black plastic bag. A final plump of the cushions on the settee and he was ready, just as the front door bell rang.

'Hello, come in,' he smiled, but the others only nodded in acknowledgement. 'Has somebody died? More like a bloody wake,' he muttered as they went through into the lounge. 'Tea all round is it? I've got some biscuits. Anybody take sugar?' he asked, trying to lighten the atmosphere.

Derek joined Gregory in the kitchen and, while the kettle boiled, they had a hushed discussion.

'This could be the last meeting,' Derek whispered. 'The rest have lost their nerve. So let's make it count. Be positive and upbeat.'

'A builder's brew and a plate of jammy dodgers. It's better than a snort of coke to liven you up, eh?' Gregory said.

False laughter broke out from the others; Derek sensed the creeping apathy and stepped in. 'Anyway, the objective is to return our businesses to winning ways. The individuals who are hindering our ability to earn an honest living have to be stopped … once and for all.'

The others offered a weak response, so Gregory tried to rouse them by offering loud support to Derek's statement. 'Hear, hear! Well said, sir,' he guffawed, as if he were in the House of Commons.

Ken, who'd been one of the first to feel the financial hit when his machines were broken into, raised his hand. 'OK, OK, let's get down to business. I believe that you have come up with yet another strategy for ridding us of the menace.'

'This time we thought we would go for Mr Big,' Gregory announced and then went on. 'Yes, I know what you're thinking but we thought that continually chasing the thief, the man on the ground so to speak, is futile. In the event that we actually catch him, he would simply be replaced.'

There was a moment of silence as the audacity of the statement sank in.

'So, this, er, Mr Big… Is that his real name?' Ken asked.

Gregory started to stutter. 'Well no, we don't know his real name.'

'And where does he live? Does he have an office? A base?'

'We're not sure about that either.'

'So let me get this straight…'

Derek jumped in to prevent Gregory from getting in a metaphorical hole. 'Ah, we do have a plan but we will need your help.' He explained that a dummy gumball machine would be used because it was light and could be carried easily. A note would be taped to it requesting help with the repair and, as an inducement, it would be full of money.

'How do you know the thief will fall for it?' Ken asked.

'Why wouldn't he? He can pick it up, money for nothing. And if he doesn't, it's cost us nothing but time.'

'So you want us to take turns watching the machine and then, if he falls for it, to alert the rest who will be in the car park?'

'Precisely.'

'And then what?'

'We follow the thief back to wherever he comes from, to Mr Big's office or workshop. After he has gone home, we can remotely detonate a small explosive hidden in the machine that will wreck his premises and show Mr Big that we mean business,' Gregory explained.

'Explosive?' said Ken, whilst trying to control a fit of coughing.

'It's only an explosive in general terms. It's not designed to hurt people, just to mess up computers, hardware or other components.

'A dirty bomb,' said John in a low tone.

'It depends on how you define dirty. The original definition was a bomb that spreads radioactive material. This doesn't, it spreads paint. It's a banger surrounded by paint balls, like you get in those paint-ball games.'

'Paint-ball games, what's he on about?' whispered Ken.

'Grown men go into the woods and shoot paint balls at one another,' John informed him.

'Really? I must be living in another world,' Ken replied, shaking his head. He turned to Gregory. 'I suppose this is your idea. You made this device?'

'It's a hobby of mine,' Gregory confirmed in a low voice.

Ken sighed audibly and held up his hands. 'Well, it costs nowt if he doesn't turn up, and if he does turn up he gets his house painted for free. Can't see anything wrong with that.'

Derek and Gregory grinned broadly whilst Ken and John forced thin smiles.

'Is this going to be alright?' Ken muttered to John as they walked through the door.

'As you said, it's not going to cost anything, so why not?'

***

Two days later, the remaining COG members put the plan into action. Wrapped up against the chill of the night, they set off with rucksacks containing flasks and sandwiches and one containing a small chewing-gum machine.

'I know just the place. The bastard's done three machines on the trot here, and it's just outside the gents so he's bound to walk past it,' said Ken, settling into the mission.

The time passed slowly. After several hours and shift changes of the lookout, the screen on Derek's phone finally lit up – but not with the information he wanted.

'If he doesn't come soon I'm off to bed. I've got work in the morning,' advised John.

'You can't go yet. He works at night, we have to give him chance.'

'Another hour then I'm off.'

The number of people in the service station reduced to a trickle. The shutters came down on most of the shops and all that was left for the weary traveller was the coffee dispenser or the distraction of a pinball machine.

It was Ken's turn to sit in the café seating area and stay alert. It was way past his bedtime, so it was no wonder that his eyes closed and his head started to drop in stages, each time closer to the table. It was the collision with the table that forced him to sit up. He rubbed his eyes then frantically dialled Derek's phone number. 'The machine's gone! It must have been while I was…'

'Asleep, you dozy git. Right, we are now looking for a man carrying a machine. Sodding hell.'

Derek clambered out of his car and met Ken running out of the front of the mall. 'He must be round the back.'

They jumped back into the car and cruised slowly round to the service area. Almost as soon as they turned into the area where refuse was processed, a car went past in the opposite direction.

'That's him, that's him!' Ken shouted from the back seat.

At the moment that the cars passed each other, both sets of occupants bowed their heads to avoid being recognised. The thief lost control of his car; it mounted the kerb, he braked hard and the car screeched to a halt. Simultaneously, John lost control of his car and it slithered into a refuse bin. Both cars were now stationary, parked awkwardly and with hot exhaust gases visible in the blazing headlights.

There was a momentary stand off as both drivers gathered their thoughts. To the thief it was a no-brainer: reverse off the kerb and set off with wheels spinning in a cloud of dust. John, in his We Vend Anything company car, was more concerned about the collision with the bin, so he opened the door to inspect the damage.

'We haven't time for that, get back in,' the others screamed.

'I'll get my arse kicked for this. I've only had the car a matter of weeks!'

The thief was unaware that the incident had other implications; he thought it was just another traffic-related occurrence and, as such, settled down to a normal cruising speed.

A three-point turn had been manoeuvred as quickly as John could achieve but the thief's car was now almost out of sight. Tempers were getting frayed.

'Get going, we're losing him!' shouted Derek from the back seat.

'But don't get too close or he will know he's being followed,' said Gregory, contradicting him.

As John hung on to the steering wheel and snatched through the gears, he turned to the others. 'So, get going or hang back. What's it to be?' he growled, getting annoyed.

'We can't lose him after all this, but we can't let him know he's being followed either. Just keep his red lights in view,' Derek ordered.

They stayed at a distance, each one straining his eyes to ensure they knew where the thief was. After many miles and numerous arguments, there was a panic as the thief turned off the main road and entered the industrial estate.

'What now?' shouted John with alarm in his voice.

'It's OK, just keep well back. This is his base, we've got the bastard now.'

Whilst keeping the car in sight, they slid in behind the hoarding that described the names of the occupants and their business.

'That must be the place,' Derek said excitedly.

'Nowt on the board that says "rotten bastard thief",' said Ken.

Once at a standstill, Derek clambered out of the car. At the same time, Gregory retrieved a small box with a red button on top from his rucksack. He pointed to it and then looked at John and Ken. 'Whatever you do, do not touch that button or bang … puff.' He demonstrated with his fingers the action of an explosion, and then laughed.

'You are proper sick,' John said with distaste.

'Probably,' Gregory replied.

Meanwhile, Derek was hiding behind the hoarding and watching the vehicle now parked outside the unit. The motion detectors had sensed its arrival and in a fleeting moment night became day as the lights blazed from above. Derek watched with interest as the occupant climbed out of the car and, with his back to him, went to the boot. He opened the lid and lifted out the gum-ball machine and, as he closed the boot lid, the bright lights shone on Geoff's face.

The hate and revenge festering inside Derek was replaced with shock and alarm as he recognised his former workmate. 'No … it can't be,' he said shaking and bursting into tears.

He turned and looked back at John's car. His mates were staring at him. His emotions were all mixed up; he felt betrayed by the man under the spotlight. It was his mate; he had worked alongside him for years. Derek just could not understand how or why – and within seconds the strain of the moment caused his legs to give way. A flood of tears ran down his face, his eyes reddened and his voice choked. 'It's my mate,' he croaked back to the others.

'What's wrong with him?' asked John with little feeling.

'Afraid he's lost it,' confirmed Ken.

John got out of the car and went to see what was going on. Derek couldn't speak; the heightened emotion had got the better of him and he just pointed. John could neither understand nor grasp the situation, and reported back to the others what he saw. 'The crook's got out of the car and now he's walking round to the front carrying the machine.' The others smiled to confirm that all was going to plan.

Then Derek crawled out from behind the hoarding and started shouting. 'Geoff, Geoff, put it down, put it down!'

Meanwhile George and Ange had been watching the goings-on on the security camera. George, followed by Ange, rushed to the door. They saw Geoff standing next to the car, still holding the machine.

'Put it down,' George screamed frantically.

'Why?' Geoff replied.

'Just put it down.'

Derek saw Geoff's hesitation. 'Put it down,' he urged.

John was relating the movements to the others in the car. 'He's putting it down,' he said, loud enough for them to hear.

Ken, who was sitting in the back of the car, couldn't stand any more. He leaned over Gregory's shoulder. 'He bleeding well isn't! He's the one that's wrecked my business,' he said angrily and he thumped the button.

As predicted, but much louder and more devastatingly, bang… puff – and Geoff went in all directions.

Gregory looked at Ken. 'Well, what did you expect? It was designed to destroy a workshop.'

John, who'd been knocked over by the blast, scrambled to his feet and ran to the driver's door. He wrenched it open and started the engine. 'I didn't join the company to get involved in this. We're out of here,' he said frantically.

The wheels of his car spun and screeched as they made their getaway, leaving Derek holding his head in his hands, sobbing on the pavement. In the blast, pound coins hit the hoarding and dropped beside him. He picked up a few, stared at them and wailed, 'This is my money. What good is it now?'

Fortunately for George, Geoff was facing away and looking towards Derek when the explosion occurred, but George still got caught in the blast of paint, pound coins and body parts. The power of the explosion threw him on his back.

Inside his workshop, Ange looked down at him. She could not believe the state he was in. 'You're dripping in something. What is it?' she said, wiping his face with a rag she found on the work bench.

As she dabbed his face, trying not to worsen the apparent major injury, she noticed pound coins embedded in his boiler suit. 'I'll get some scissors. We'll have to cut this off you.'

She carefully cut down the arms and legs of George's boiler suit then dragged the sopping material away from him. Red dots appeared on his shirt where the coins that had flown like bullets had hit him. She helped him to his feet and, after a minute or two, he told her the next move. 'We are out of here. Shortly there will be lots of people asking very serious questions. You and I cannot get involved.'

'What about Geoff?' she asked softly.

'Geoff has gone.' George put it simply.

Ange's head pointed towards the floor and a tear dripped from her nose.

George let the news sink in, then handed her a tissue and pointed towards a fire alarm button on the wall. 'Unfortunately, time is not on our side. We have to get moving. That button over there – hit it, will you?'

'It says in the event of an emergency,' she queried.

'This *is* an emergency. Please hit it.'

She left George leaning on the work bench, went to the wall and pressed the button. Immediately smoke came out of the back of the computer. 'What about all this?' she asked, looking round the walls.

'It's just a workshop … I can set one up anywhere.'

'Barcelona?'

'Anywhere.'

'And the tea caddies?' she pondered.

'From what Geoff told me, it's perhaps best if we don't set foot anywhere near the place.'

'No secrets then?'

'No.'

A job well done?

Digger and Spade were completing the detailed reports on the investigation into the chemical factory deaths.

'Are you going to mention your nightmare?' Spade asked, laughing.

'Do you know, I can still smell that rubber. I think it's on the end of my nose. OK, I won't mention my nightmare so long as you keep your shoes and socks on.'

They gathered up the scraps of paper from the evidence board and the envelope containing the picture of the severed head. 'No, don't open it. I can still see it in my mind,' begged Spade.

Digger paused for a moment then rifled at the bottom of an envelope for a scrap of paper. 'Here, I found this under the windscreen the last time we were there. I haven't thrown it away yet. I thought you should see it first.'

He passed the note over to Spade, who read it out loud. '"Your officer is knocking about with a secretary in our office. We are currently under investigation. Is this ethical under the circumstances?"'

'Tell me you're not,' Digger said.

'I'm not,' Spade replied.

'That will do me. I knew you couldn't be that daft.' Digger chuckled as he screwed up the note and threw it in the bin.

On successful completion of an investigation, it was customary that the officers involved were presented with a large tin of biscuits for them and the rest of the staff to consume during the mid-morning tea break.

The presentation was well underway as their superior officer entered the crowded office and looked around for his men. Protocol dictated that it was Digger's duty to offer the boss the open tin to choose from.

'Yes, a job well done, Digger and Spade,' Chief Inspector Peacock groaned, as though the words were broken glass in his throat. 'I don't mind if I do,' he said, selecting a fig biscuit from under the custard creams. At that moment a secretary opened the door and indicated to the boss that there was a phone call for him. 'Excuse me, gentlemen, won't be a mo.'

The gallows' humour was in full swing; the nature of the case had not been lost on the other officers. 'The headless two investigated by the brainless two,' was written on their evidence board, plus several unhelpful references to 'body wash and facial scrub'.

As the boss re-entered the room, it was obvious something was up and the raucous laughter halted immediately. He moved smartly forward, took hold of the box of biscuits and closed the lid.

'Sorry, gentlemen, party's over ... they've found another head.'

Who'd have thought it?

A few months later, a bronzed gentleman walked smartly in through the front door of The Crown village pub. It was Friday lunchtime and he expected the clamour of voices and the smell of real ale and wholesome food. The landlord was busy cleaning the bar and washing glasses, and didn't notice the first customer of the day. The man stood, amazed at the lack of clientele; disappointment was written across his face as he spun around holding out his palms in a theatrical gesture of surprise. 'Crikey, what's happened here?'

'Oh hello. Can I get you a table? Will you be eating with us?' asked the now-attentive landlord. He studied the bronzed gentleman then, in a more local accent, exclaimed, 'Hey, it's you, isn't it? The last time I saw you, you were crying in your beer.' In a much lower tone, he continued, 'We all thought you'd drowned – at least, that was the rumour.'

'No, I just got on a plane. Inside twenty-four hours, I was in a bar in Malaga. Been working there ever since. I should have done it sooner. Anyway, I'll have a pint accompanied by your very finest meat pie and peas. I've told all my mates in Malaga how good they are. I can't wait.'

The landlord tilted his head to one side and apologised. 'Very sorry. The factory closed down so we had to change the menu. The nearest I can get to pie and peas is beef Wellington wrapped in filo pastry, with a portion of oven-roasted seasonal vegetables and a gravy boat of red wine jus.'

'Er … no thanks.'

About the Author

Colin Goodwin enjoyed a successful career as a welding and fabrication engineer, working for the past twenty years in further education, where he also taught stained glass window making.

Recently retired, he is continuing to indulge his creative side by repairing anything mechanical (motor bikes, cars, model steam engines). *Nightmare on the Nightshift* is his latest book after *Don't Get Mad Get Even* and it's sequel *When in a hole, Stop Digging*. Colin lives in Lancashire.